DATE			

THE LAST LAWMEN

Also by the Author

THE LAST LAWMEN

Jack Cummings

Walker and Company
New York

All the characters and events portrayed in this work are fictitious.

First published in the United States of America in 1994 by Walker Publishing
Company, Inc.

Published simultaneously in Canada by Thomas Allen & Son Canada, Limited,
Markham, Ontario

Library of Congress Cataloging-in-Publication Data
Cummings, Jack, 1925–
The last lawmen / Jack Cummings.
p.   cm.
ISBN 0-8027-4143-6
I. Title.
PS3553.U444L37   1994
813'.54—dc20   94-8811
CIP

Printed in the United States of America

2 4 6 8 10 9 7 5 3 1

AUTHOR'S NOTE

Arizona Territory in 1901 was still Old West.

The Apache threat was gone, but in its place had come a horde of outlaws seeking, in this wild and sparsely settled terrain, a refuge from advancing civilization.

Badmen from everywhere poured in—to plunder, rustle, kill, and rape. In desperation, the Territorial governor sought a force to combat these predators.

And thus was born the Arizona Rangers. For seven years they rode horseback wherever needed, and shot it out whenever guns were drawn.

They were the last of the frontier lawmen, as tough and hard and courageous as any who had gone before.

And only a few of them tarnished the silver star they wore.

THE LAST LAWMEN

CHAPTER 1

Morenci, Arizona Territory, June 9, 1903

THE REPORTER, JUST one of many in town to cover the week-old miners' labor strike, was eating breakfast alone in the Hotel Brisco when he overheard a discussion that caught his interest.

Two of the mining town's merchants were eating at the table adjacent to his. They were talking about a couple of Arizona Rangers who yesterday had killed three bank robbers—an incident exciting in itself, but eclipsed by the story of the uneasy relationship between the rangers.

One had said, "It beats all how those two rangers are so often thrown together whenever there's trouble."

"Like yesterday afternoon," his companion said.

"The rumor is Wes Barnes and Jake Kenton hate each other's guts. Goes far back. Couple of years maybe."

"I heard they've known each other a long time. One saved the other's life. Then the other reciprocated. That's how it began, way I heard it. I've met Barnes. Seemed like a fair-minded lawman."

"That's what makes it strange. Kenton is the opposite. Got a heavy-handed way of enforcing his brand of law. Been hauled in and chewed out by the ranger captain about it more than once. It's badge toters like him can cause the rangers a lot of criticism, in spite of the guts most of them show in chasing down rustlers and bandits, and shooting it out with hard-case killers in saloons and bad-lands."

The reporter's curiosity was aroused about the mis-matched pair. He had an impulse to intrude on the speak-

1

ers, but it was too late: they rose from their finished meal and exited.

He was left with an unfinished breakfast and a craving to know more about the two rangers they had been discussing.

He decided to use his day making some inquiries.

By midday he knew enough to feel ready to seek an interview with Barnes and Kenton. But separately, of course.

He had learned that the shoot-out at the bank had nothing directly to do with the reason the rangers were there.

They had been sent in, along with others, because of the trouble between the miners and the mine operators over wages.

The bank shooting was pure happenstance. Barnes and Kenton had approached the site separately, walking from opposite directions. Across the street, the trio of robbers ran out of the bank, carrying a sack with forty thousand dollars in currency.

Both rangers got the picture at once and opened fire together.

Two of the robbers were mortally wounded; the third raised his hands, not even drawing his gun.

Barnes was covering him, but did not fire again. Kenton, however, took careful and unhurried aim, and put a bullet into the surrendering outlaw's face. The bullet tore away the back of his head.

Wes Barnes swore.

The two rangers closed in then, Barnes with a sick, bitter expression. When they neared each other, Barnes said, "He was giving up, dammit!"

"I made sure he did," Kenton said, grinning like a Cheshire cat. "For keeps."

The reporter found Barnes seated alone, having dinner in the Brisco. It was the wrong time to bother the man, and he knew it. But he had discovered that impetuosity sometimes brought unexpected results, and he decided to risk an approach.

"Mr. Barnes?"

The ranger looked up, swallowed a mouthful of beef.

"Yes? What is it?" Barnes's eyes swept the reporter's clothes, saw no sign of a weapon. He met his glance then and held it, waiting.

"May I interview you, sir?"

"You got nerve, son, to interrupt a man while he's eating."

Barnes was a lean and tough-looking man of maybe not yet thirty, and to be called son by him irritated the reporter just enough to make him rash.

"I was afraid I'd miss you later," he said.

A trace of a smile broke the hard lines of Barnes's face. "Well, in that case, I suppose I ought to listen. Sit down."

"Thank you," the reporter said, sitting in the chair across from Barnes. "My name is William Moran, Mr. Barnes." He paused, then asked his first question. "How did you happen to team up with Mr. Kenton?"

Barnes frowned slightly. "Team up? You mean during the shooting yesterday?"

The reporter shook his head, then said, "Well, that too, I suppose. But I've heard it's happened before. Frequently, as a matter of fact."

"So it has," Barnes said.

"Why?"

"*Why?*"

"I mean, how is it that it happens this way?"

"I don't know," Barnes said slowly. He looked at him squarely and said, "But tell me, do you believe in chance?"

"Of course I do. But the odds of you and Kenton being thrown together so often purely by chance seems to be higher than the law of averages."

Barnes picked at his food for a moment, then said, "That may be but, dammit, that's all it can be! I didn't know he would be walking down the street yesterday and I sure as hell didn't know there was going to be a bank robbery."

"Intriguing, though," the reporter said. "Especially since word is there's little friendship between you."

Barnes was silent.

"Am I right?"

Barnes nodded. "True."

"When did you and Kenton first meet?"

"We met a couple of years ago. Down in Mexico. Neither of us was a lawman then."

"Can you tell me about it?"

"I can. But I don't know if I will."

The reporter was smart enough to wait without speaking.

That made Barnes ask, "Why should I?"

"No reason, except I asked."

The lawman laid down his fork and stared into his plate.

When the ranger did not speak the reporter said, "I might ask what each of you was doing in Mexico."

"We had our reasons."

"Of course."

"I never did know what Kenton was doing down there before I met him," Barnes said. "Me, it was simple enough. I had taken a guard's job at an American-owned Mexican mine. A band of bronco Yaquis were raising particular hell about that time down there."

The reporter said, "I heard they'd been fighting the Mexican government off and on for years."

"This was different. The poor bastards were starving— bad weather for their meager crops on their *rancherias*. Think of this: their first raid was on the mine company's commissary, not a payroll shipment."

"You drove them off?"

"I hate to say it, but I did. Wounded a couple out of a

band of six, but then held my fire so they all could get away."

The reporter thought about this, but said nothing.

"The mine manager didn't take too well to my performance."

"He wanted more wounded?"

"Wanted them all dead," Barnes said.

"I see. And how did you meet Kenton?"

"The mining company brought him in."

"He took your job?"

Barnes shook his head. "They kept the both of us."

"How long did that last?"

"Not long," Barnes said. "Not for me. I left."

"Because of Kenton?"

Barnes hesitated. Then he said, "That had some bearing on it."

"A clash of personalities, then?"

"Yes."

"And he—?"

"The feeling is mutual, if that's what you're asking," Barnes said.

"So you left. When did you meet up again?"

"Last year. When we joined the rangers."

"You joined together?"

"Hell, no! Captain Ryerson signed me up in Douglas, and Kenton a few days before, in Naco."

"Each unaware of the other's enlistment?"

"That's right."

"Came as a surprise, then, when you next met?"

"As you can imagine," Barnes said. "I don't think Cap Ryerson knew we were acquainted. If he did, he didn't know how it was between us. Not at that time. Because he ordered us both up to Dragoon to stop a lot of hell-raising that was going on. Just the two of us, as *partners*.

"What happened there was, we no more than reached the town and stopped in the nearest saloon when Kenton got into an argument with the saloon owner. He wanted to know what we were doing in his place of business.

" 'Get the hell out!' he said. 'I don't want no damned rangers scaring off my customers.' "

Barnes told the reporter Jake Kenton took offense at the verbal abuse of the saloon keeper, a rough customer named Sawyer. Kenton whipped out his six-gun and slammed its barrel against Sawyer's temple.

Sawyer, a stocky, powerful figure, did not go down. He staggered back and bumped a table where a couple of men were drinking. Sawyer grabbed a nearly full quart bottle from the table and smashed it into Kenton's face.

Kenton shot the saloon owner in the shoulder, which did put Sawyer on the floor, blood pouring from the wound.

Barnes grabbed Kenton's arm just as he pointed his gun down at the wounded man.

The town marshal had heard the shot from out on the street and rushed in. He saw Sawyer down, the two rangers standing there, one gripping the other's gun arm, and he raised a shotgun he was carrying.

"Hold it there!" he shouted.

Kenton twisted at the sound, saw the Greener, and holstered his pistol. He called out, "This is ranger business, marshal!"

"Not now, it ain't," the marshal said. "Drop your guns, both of you, till I sort this out."

Kenton hesitated as Barnes obeyed, then grudgingly followed suit.

But as he did, he said, "Barnes, don't ever grab my arm like that again."

There was some disagreement among the half-drunk witnesses as to who brought on the shooting, and when it turned out that Sawyer's wound was little more than a grazing flesh wound, the marshal, Jed Grant, who had served briefly as a ranger himself in 1901 under then-captain, Burt Mossman, refused to arrest Kenton.

There was resentment and grumbling by some of the saloon denizens, and an expression of outrage from Sawyer.

But Marshal Grant, who considered Sawyer's dive a source of trouble in the town, ignored his protest. He was inclined to welcome the presence of the rangers in a town that was getting too hot for him to handle.

And the incident in the saloon, and the presence of the two new lawmen patroling on horseback, had its effect. The amount of raucous crime lessened in a matter of days.

Kenton gloated. "Way to treat these bastards," he said to Barnes.

"I ain't so sure," Barnes said, remembering Kenton standing over the downed saloon keeper, pistol pointed at Sawyer's head.

He was almost certain Kenton would have pulled the trigger, had he not grabbed his arm. As he recalled his earlier contact with Kenton at the mine in Mexico, he was damned sure of it.

After a week, they left Dragoon. They had received orders to head into the area east of the Santa Rita Mountains, where it was reported a pair of apparent army deserters had held up a stage station and could be hiding in the surrounding country.

They reached the scene on the Crittenden–Pantano stage line and got a firsthand account from the agent there.

"Two young hardcases in dirty Army clothes, and bad need of a shave," the station keeper told them, "took the only two saddle-broke horses I had here, and sacks of foodstuffs, much as they could tie on." He paused. "They was armed with Army Colt revolvers."

"They arrive on foot?" Kenton said.

"Nope," the agent said. "Look there in the corral at them two army mounts. Them horses was in bad shape from hard riding when they got here. Fresh animals and grub is what those bandits needed. Took all the cash they could find or scare me out of, too."

"Deserters, huh?" Kenton said.

"Army horses, McClellan saddles, soldier clothes," the station keeper said. "What else?"

"I hate the breed," Kenton said.

"Deserters?"

"Yeah."

The station keeper gave him an appraising stare, but all he said was, "First time I ever run into any."

Kenton didn't comment further.

Barnes said, "What direction did they take when they left here?"

"North," the agent said. "Nearest town is Clayton, ten or so miles. My guess is they might've had in mind to buy some civilian clothes, soon as they could."

"Makes sense," Barnes said. "They could be from Fort Huachuca. If so, it ain't likely they'd head back that way."

"My thinking, too," the station keeper said. He paused, then said, "You know, they seemed hardly more than kids, rough as they looked from trail grime. Talked with a back East accent, kind of. I got the feeling they might've enlisted to come West, looking for adventure, and probably found the army life didn't agree with them."

Barnes said to the station man, "We'll care for our horses, then push on."

"Sure," the agent said.

They reached the town, and by custom stopped at a saloon. Experience had taught them that saloons were the headquarters for local news, rumors or otherwise. From such gleanings, they hoped to pick up the trail of their quarry.

Standing at the bar with their first drink, they twisted about to survey the few scattered patrons. It was not yet noon, and these were few.

Barnes was about to turn back to interrogate the barkeep when his interest fastened on a clean-shaven pair in new range clothes, seated at a table, a bottle between them.

The bottle was already half empty.

He nudged Kenton.

Kenton gave the two a brief study, then said, "Let's go!"

Together they approached the table.

"New clothes," Kenton muttered.

"Not armed," Barnes said.

"Makes it easy then, don't it?" Kenton said.

As they neared, the eyes of the pair raised toward them, and Barnes thought he saw a sign of alarm there as they focused on the ranger badges.

"Like to talk to you boys," Barnes said.

"Sure," one of them said. "Have a drink while you do."

Kenton said, "There's some kinds I don't drink with."

"Your choice," the kid said.

"You damn right it is. And I hate a goddamned deserter."

The other youngster said, "What do you mean— deserter?"

Barnes said, "You boys working hereabouts?"

"That's right."

"Yeah?" Kenton said. "Who for?"

"Cherrycow Cattle Company, that's who."

"They pay you to sit here and drink, do they?"

"We been doing some Sunday work, and they give us a day off for doing it."

"Your duds look brand new," Kenton said.

"Ain't quite. But we save them for when we come to town."

"Got a lot of answers, ain't you?" Kenton said.

"I thought that's what you were after."

"Where's your guns?"

"What guns?"

"The ones you use to hold up stage stations with," Kenton said. "Them Army Colts you took when you deserted."

"Man," the other kid said, "you got us confused with somebody else."

He was the one sitting nearest to Kenton, and Kenton drew his gun and slammed him with it above the ear, just as he had done to the saloon owner in Dragoon.

The kid fell over sideways, slumped on the tabletop.

Barnes began to swear.

The barkeep came running from behind the bar and said, "What the hell did you do that for?"

"He had a smart mouth I didn't like," Kenton said.

"Hell," the barkeep said. "Both these boys are regular customers. Been so for over a year that I been here. Work for a big ranch hereabouts."

"Why didn't you say so?" Kenton said.

"You didn't ask me."

The kid slumped on the table began to stir. He raised his head and stared dazedly at Kenton.

Kenton looked at him without expression. "Listen, you," he said, "when somebody wearing this ranger badge asks you something, you answer 'yes, sir, no, sir.' You understand?"

The kid mumbled, "I ain't ever been in the army."

"My mistake," Kenton said.

The barkeep said, "You looking for deserters? There was a couple, looked like they could've been stopped here on their way through, three, four days ago. Drunk some likker, asked about where's a clothing store."

"They go to buy some?"

"Don't think so. About that time our town constable walked in. They saw him and walked out. I remember I was curious and stepped to the door to watch them. It appeared they rode right out of town. Headed north. Leastwise I haven't seen them around since."

Kenton said, "You could have saved this boy here a bad headache had you spoke up sooner."

"Hell, man, I can't read minds."

Barnes said, "They got quite a lead."

The barkeep nodded. "Yeah. But there's other mining settlements up ahead they might have lingered at."

"My thinking, too," Barnes said.

The kid that Kenton had hit kept staring at him in a stunned sort of way. There was blood running out of his left ear below where he'd been clouted.

Kenton started to speak, then seemed to change his mind, and turned away, heading for the door.

Barnes said, "I'm sorry, son. He gets a little out of hand sometimes."

The other kid said, "I hope somebody kills the bastard!"

"Maybe they will," Barnes said. He turned then and followed Kenton out.

They reached a cattle town ten miles up the trail, There wasn't much there—just a store, a blacksmith and livery, a small restaurant, and a small saloon.

There was not even a sign in sight to give the place a name.

Again they hitched in front of the board-fronted bar structure.

There was a difference here: behind the bar was a middle-aged woman. She was sitting on a stool, reading a newspaper. She did not look up as they came in.

They crossed the few paces to the bar, and Kenton said, "Hey!"

She looked up then, and the ranger stars on their shirts seemed to catch her attention briefly before she met their eyes.

"Afternoon, ma'am," Barnes said.

"Well," she said, "you ain't far behind them."

"Behind who, ma'am?" Barnes said.

"Ain't you after them two deserters I'm reading about here in this paper? Busted out of the guardhouse at Fort Huachuca a few days back?"

"Matter of fact we are, ma'am."

Kenton said, "I take it they stopped here?"

"Thought they'd never leave," the woman said. "Had some money and spent it, so they didn't bother me much at first. But they got drunk and stayed drunk most of two days and a night. Got downright obnoxious after a while, particularly when I stopped putting out the free lunch they was living on."

"Bother your other customers, did they?" Barnes said.

"I don't have many during the weekdays, but, yes, they drove them off, after a while. But they was spending enough to make it worthwhile. At first, anyhow."

"They run out of money?" Barnes asked.

"No, that ain't what I mean. What I mean is their money got to where it wasn't worth the aggravation they was causing me."

"Reckon that could happen," Barnes said.

"At first they was kind of polite. Both of them addressed me as ma'am, just like you do. But along about the second day one of them changed that to *madam*, as if I was running a whorehouse or something. I guess he thought that was funny, but I didn't.

"Anyhow, I was glad when they rode out of town this morning."

"Heading north?" Barnes said.

"Only way the road runs," the woman said. "Except for south, which is where they come from."

Kenton said, "We'll be closing in on them, then. They'll wish they'd never deserted when we do."

The woman stared at him, then an uneasy expression came over her well-worn face as she said, "Well, hell, they really wasn't bad boys, even here. As to them deserting, I understand the army causes a lot of men to do the same."

Kenton's own hard stare met hers. "A man deserts, he should be shot," he said.

CHAPTER 2

THEY RODE ON, following the horse tracks they'd picked up in front of the saloon. The roadway was hard-packed after a few miles, and the hoofprints no longer showed.

Barnes said, "They could have turned off anywheres."

"Not likely, unless it's on a trail."

"Yeah."

But after a while Barnes began to have his doubts. He was about to mention them, when he saw the discarded whiskey bottle gleaming in the sun a few yards off the left side of the road.

"Look there!" he said, reining up.

Kenton halted too. "Still drinking?"

Barnes said, "Hair of the dog. They brought it along for their hangovers. After a two- or three-day binge, they could be a couple of sick sons of bitches."

"Might make them easier to handle."

"Or harder," Barnes said.

Kenton shrugged. "Either way," he said. He kicked his mount, moving on as if anxious to close in. Barnes followed, thinking, He's taking this case like it's personal.

A couple of hours later they came upon signs of a rest stop.

Horse sign indicated it had lasted awhile.

Barnes said, "Hangover got too much for them maybe."

"Let's get on with it," Kenton said. His voice sounded impatient.

The road led through a narrow canyon between some rocky hills.

Barnes halted, studying the cut.

Kenton said, "What're you waiting for? We got only one way to go."

"Good place for an ambush."

"Come on," Kenton said. "Them bastards don't know we're behind them. If they did, they wouldn't have slept back there along the roadway."

"Reckon you're right," Barnes said, and gigged his horse as Kenton pushed into the chasm.

A little later he said, "You've been a soldier, I understand. You think they'll give up without a fight?"

"I hope not," Kenton said.

Barnes was about to ask why. But at that moment, a revolver blasted from a screen of rocks in a bend directly ahead. A bullet passed them and ricocheted off a rock behind them.

They turned and dove into the cover of boulders at the road edge, but in their urgency ended up on opposite sides.

That was just as well, Barnes thought.

Kenton called out, "There's your answer!"

He sounded pleased.

What was there to be pleased about? Barnes thought. It was hot in the canyon, and they appeared to be stymied there until, or unless, the deserters chose to move on. He had been right to worry about an ambush.

Then Kenton called again, but not so loudly, "Barnes, you give me covering fire. You hear?"

"What for?"

"Hell, man, I'm not letting those gutless bastards stop me."

Barnes saw him swing into his saddle, high enough now to be a target for the ambushers.

A couple of shots came from the hidden men.

"Cover me, I said!" Kenton yelled, and a moment later he spurred his way into a mounted charge.

Barnes did his best. He threw four successive shots at the glimpses he had of the enemy rising slightly to fire.

Then Kenton burst through an opening in their natural rampart, twisted in his saddle, and opened up with his handgun.

Barnes heard one of them cry out in pain. Then the firing stopped.

He leaped into his own saddle and reached Kenton's side just in time to see one man on the ground, unmoving, and the second deserter with hands raised, gun dropped, and Kenton aiming at his gut.

"For chrissakes, don't shoot!" Barnes said.

"Why not?"

"That's murder!"

"He's a deserter," Kenton said. "I'm a firing squad."

"You're crazy," Barnes said.

And at that moment, the man on the ground moved slightly to grasp a dropped weapon. He raised it surprisingly high and shot it half-blindly, striking Barnes low on his left side. Barnes slumped, grabbing for the saddle horn with one hand and grabbing at his holster with the other.

He heard the blast of Kenton's gun, saw the body-jerk of the prone assailant as the bullet drilled his head.

The other deserter dropped his hands and snatched at the Army Colt lying at his feet. He was almost straightened up when Kenton's shot took him just above the breastbone.

He never moved again.

Barnes saw it all, still clutching the horn to keep from falling.

He turned his eyes to Kenton.

Kenton caught his stare, and said, "You hit bad?"

"I don't know."

"You'd have been worse off if that bastard had got off another shot."

"I guess."

Kenton dismounted, dropped his reins, and moved over to him. "Let's get you out of the saddle and have a look."

With his help, Barnes managed to get off his horse.

He sprawled out, and Kenton studied his wound. "Took a chunk of meat out of you, is all. We get the blood stopped and a bandage on, you'll be able to ride, though it'll hurt like hell."

Barnes looked over at the other figures lying on the ground.

"Both dead?" he said.

"Yeah," Kenton said. "A damned good day's work."

Barnes turned his eyes back to Kenton's face.

It showed him nothing.

Neither of them spoke while Kenton improvised a compress from Barnes's neckerchief and tied it over the flesh wound.

"I'll give you a boost into your saddle," Kenton said then.

"What about those bodies?"

"Leave them lay. Their horses run off, spooked by the shooting. We'll leave word when we get back to that mining town. They can send out a wagon if they're so inclined. Let's ride."

Barnes stood up, walked to his horse, and got into his saddle without asking help from Jake.

He kept thinking, *A good day's work?*

CHAPTER 3

WES BARNES SAT in the Hotel Brisco dining room, surprised by how much he had told the reporter.

"Listen," Barnes said, "if you write this up in some kind of a story, go a little easy on him. Him and me don't see eye to eye on a lot of things, but even so, he may have saved me from being killed by that wounded deserter."

The reporter said, "He very well may have. And the story is in your difference of attitudes, not necessarily on the harshness of his methods. This is a hard country. Maybe his way is what it'll take to tame it."

Barnes said, "I've thought of that. The Territorial Assembly has passed an act to increase the ranger force from fourteen to twenty-six men: one captain, one lieutenant, four sergeants, and twenty of us privates. But that ain't a hell of a lot for the territory we have to cover."

The reporter nodded again. "You're right, there. And what's your pay?"

"Just raised to a hundred dollars a month."

"Not much for what you do."

"Beats what I used to make as a cowhand, which was what I was doing when I joined up."

"Even so."

"Yeah, even so, when you figure we furnish our own horse and weapons. We mostly use Colt .45 handguns and the 1895 Winchester 30-40 rifle specified by Burt Mossman when he organized the outfit in the beginning."

"Why that model?"

17

"Great weapon," Barnes said. "And another advantage, it takes the same cartridge as the army Krag-Jorgensen. We roam far out in the back country sometimes, running down rustlers or other owlhoots. If we get low on ammo, we can draw from a fort's quartermaster, if there's one in the area."

"An important point, I'd guess."

"Believe it," Barnes said. He paused. "You going to try to get Kenton's point of view on how it is?"

"I had it in mind. You think I can?"

Barnes shrugged. "I know him as well as anybody. But I couldn't say. You've probably gathered from what I've said that he's a closemouthed son of a bitch about his actions."

"Well, I intend to try, and I want to thank you for granting me this interview."

"Good luck," Barnes said. His eyes followed the reporter as he crossed toward the door.

He felt a little uneasy about telling the reporter as much as he had. Might be better, he was thinking now, if I was closemouthed as Kenton is.

The trouble was the damn reporter was a good listener.

That didn't seem to help much when he encountered Kenton on the street.

"Mr. Kenton?"

Kenton's glance took him in, head to foot, before he spoke. "Yeah?"

"I'm a reporter, down here to cover the mine conflict."

Kenton said, "And I'm here to help see nothing gets out of hand. That's about all I got to say about it."

"I understand how you feel, but it wasn't the mine trouble I wanted to ask you about."

"So? What else could it be?"

Like Barnes, Kenton had a lean, tough look about him,

but he was a little stockier in build. Muscle, though, not fat. His face was hard, looked as if he didn't smile much.

"It was more about the shoot-out at the bank robbery."

Kenton's face seemed to lighten a little. "Oh, that. What's the question?"

"I understand you and Mr. Barnes have been partners before during similar actions."

"Couple of times, or so."

"You work well together?"

"You heard what happened in front of the bank. How would you judge it?"

"One of the robbers was trying to surrender, I understand."

"What difference does that make? He'd just robbed the bank. Hell, it was him was carrying the sack of money."

"Had his hands in the air, though."

"He'd just committed a crime. That's what us rangers are for. To stamp out the crime that's got too big in the Territory."

"You figure it was your duty to shoot him?"

"Sure way to end one criminal, wasn't it?"

"It doesn't bother you to shoot an unarmed man?"

"Not if he's a criminal. You got something against that?"

"Not every man would feel that way."

"Not every man is a ranger."

"Not every ranger would, either."

"Then they just might be in the wrong business," Kenton said.

"I haven't the experience to judge that. You're probably right."

Kenton's hard visage lightened a little more. "You may have more sense than a lot of these other reporters hanging around here. You can be damn sure I'm right."

"And how do you appraise your partner?"

Kenton's face hardened again. "If you ask that, maybe you ain't as smart as I thought."

"I mean as a fighting man."

"Fair man with a six-gun. Crack shot with a rifle."

"That's not exactly what I meant."

Kenton stared at him, then said, "You mean because he's not like me when it comes to killing?"

"Bluntly, yes."

"Your interview is over," Kenton replied, then turned and walked away.

The mine trouble that had brought the rangers into the area was a strike. The mine workers were demanding an eight-hour-shift wage of $2.50. The local mine company officials were offering only $2.25. The miners struck.

The politically influential mine owners called for the presence of the rangers to forestall possible violence. The governor's office sent orders to the ranger headquarters in Douglas.

Barnes, Kenton, and over a dozen other rangers soon arrived by train. They were led by Cap Ryerson himself, who set up a command post in a hotel, not the Brisco.

There they learned that three thousand miners had walked off their jobs and were encamped at various locales around the town.

Surprisingly, the presence of the rangers seemed to hold at bay any widespread violence by the vastly greater force of strikers.

After four days of a tense situation, interspersed by a few relatively minor incidents, other forces summoned by the political clout of the mine owners arrived on the scene.

First was a two-hundred-plus member Arizona National Guard unit. A short time later three troops of cavalry rode in from Fort Huachuca.

It was decided the rangers had served their purpose, forestalling by their presence the threat of action by the overwhelming number of irate miners. Confronted by a battalion-sized military force, the mine workers succumbed, accepted what the operators offered, and went back to work.

The rangers were leaving without regret. They had prevented mob violence, but it was a duty they had done reluctantly. Hunting down outlaws was their calling, they felt. Strikebreaking was not.

The story of the aborted bank robbery made the pages of the town newspaper, with the local editor's comment that several witnesses had remarked on the unneeded killing of at least one of the robbers. The story appeared on the morning that Cap Ryerson was assembling his contingent to debark.

The reporter, a copy of the paper under his arm, had the temerity to broach Ryerson as he was abandoning his field headquarters at the hotel.

Ryerson recalled seeing him among a gathering of other newsmen. The captain was a man conscious that good press relations, whenever they could be had, were advantageous to his company of lawmen.

"If I might have a brief word with you, sir?" the reporter asked.

"Yes, but I hope you can keep it short," Ryerson said.

The reporter unfolded the copy of the twice-weekly paper to show the caption concerning the killing of the bank holdup men.

The ranger captain nodded. "Yes, I've read the piece."

"Any comments, sir?"

"My men did a job they are trained to do."

"No argument there, but it appears that one of the outlaws was attempting to surrender."

"That's possible."

"There were witnesses who have stated so."

"The witnesses," the ranger captain said, "were not under fire."

"Neither were the two rangers."

Ryerson frowned. "Have you ever been in a shoot-out?"

"No, sir."

Ryerson said quietly, "Then you cannot understand how it is when gunfire erupts around you. Your adrenaline takes over. Any combat man can tell you that."

"But the bullets here were going only one way. Two men were down, mortally wounded, the other trying to surrender."

"They had just robbed a bank," Ryerson said. "For all my men knew, there were more robbers coming out of the bank behind them or covering them in a nearby alley. The fact that this didn't turn out to be the case doesn't matter."

"Barnes withheld his fire. Kenton didn't."

"Different backgrounds and different instincts," Ryerson said. "Kenton has been in a lot more dangerous situations. He fought valiantly in Cuba. We have other rangers who were there."

"But the war did not affect them all like Kenton, would you say?"

Ryerson shrugged. "I can't say whether it affected him or not. But he is, all in all, an effective ranger. He gets done any job I send him on."

"But why do you pair him with Barnes? They appear to be incompatible."

"My feeling," the ranger captain said, "is that they complement each other."

"You make allowances for Kenton's action at the bank, then?"

Ryerson was silent for a long moment. Then he said, "I make allowances for him."

The reporter had taken enough of the captain's time, and said, "Thanks for talking to me, sir."

"Keep in mind," Ryerson said, "that we rangers are doing our best to combat the outlawry that's taken over the Territory."

"I am well aware of that."

Ryerson started off, then turned back briefly to say, "You know, I took part in the charge up San Juan Hill myself." He then strode over to where the waiting rangers stood, some conversing, some silent.

The reporter noticed that Barnes and Kenton stood on opposite sides of the group, as far away from each other as possible—an indication of a renewed strain between them, perhaps heightened by the editorial slant of that morning's paper. It made him wonder if Ryerson would take notice of this, and if he did, would it change his mind about continuing to pair them.

As the train pulled out for Douglas, he realized he had no way of knowing.

A few days later, the ranger captain called the two into his office. He waved them into a couple of chairs, then stood behind his battered desk, silently staring at them.

Ryerson was a tall, impressive man, built like a greyhound.

Barnes was relieved when Ryerson sat down and spoke. He had been expecting comment about the bank affair, but the captain made none.

Instead he said, "Your next assignment will be to investigate some cattle rustling over in Santa Cruz County."

Barnes came close to asking, "Together?" But he held it back.

The answer was obvious. Why else would they both be here?

Kenton said, "What's going on over there?"

Ryerson shrugged. "That's for you to find out—and put a stop to. A cattle rancher over there reports a heavy loss recently."

"Any sign of where they're being sold?" Barnes said. "A few years back, there was some running-iron branded stock being offered to Fort Huachuca."

"Army put a stop to that. Nothing like it recently.

There's some Mexican beef driven up and sold cheap there, but that's not our problem." He paused. "Beef going the other way is."

"Into Mexico?" Barnes said.

"Mexican ranchers down there are glad to get stolen beef if the price is cheap."

Barnes and Kenton both were silent, then finally Barnes asked the question. "Suppose we're trailing a bunch of rustling drovers, and we come to the border. Ain't it against the international boundary treaty for us to enter Mexico in pursuit?"

Kenton gave a derisive snort, but remained otherwise silent.

Ryerson gave him a studying look. "You wouldn't consider that a problem, Jake?"

"Not at all, Cap," Kenton said.

"I figured you wouldn't," Ryerson said. "But to answer your question, Barnes, since I took command of the company I've been seeking to get closer cooperation with the Mexican officials. And I've got it, I think. I've met in Naco with Colonel Emilio Kosterlitzky, chief of the *Rurales,* the Mexican state rural police, and he has come to realize this will work to both our advantages. Provided we don't go too far into the interior."

"How far?" Kenton said.

"Nothing specified," the captain said.

"Good!" Kenton said. "I like it that way."

Barnes frowned. "Be better if we knew a limit, maybe."

Ryerson looked thoughtful, then said, "I'd say a full day's ride would be permissible. Something like that."

A faint grin touched Kenton's face. "Yes, sir," he said. "*Something like that* could be just about right, Captain."

Ryerson pretended to ignore his statement.

Instead, he said, "There's one other thing about this rancher who lost the cattle. She's a woman."

Barnes and Kenton each gave him a look of curiosity.

"A woman rancher?" Barnes said.

"You've heard of such, haven't you?"

"Of course," Barnes said. "Kind of a surprise, is all. Not too many of them around."

"Could be interesting," Kenton said.

CHAPTER 4

A FEW DAYS of hard riding took them into the northwest corner of Santa Cruz County, from where had come the report of the recent rustler activity.

They stopped at an isolated settlement, a small clutch of adobe buildings, one of which bore the sign *Elgin Mercantile.*

The country here was high, rolling grassland.

Barnes said, "Fine grazing."

Kenton rode to the front of the store, making no comment.

They dismounted and tied to the hitchrack before he spoke.

"Makes for fine cattle. Rustler's paradise. What was the name of that rancher reported her loss to headquarters?"

"Covell. Jane Covell."

They entered the place. It looked like the inside of a thousand other stores in the West.

The storekeeper came from a rear room as he heard them.

He, too, looked like a thousand others of his kind, Barnes thought. And his eyes took in the stars they wore.

He said then, "Glad to see you, Rangers."

Barnes nodded. "Know a rancher named Covell?"

"Sure do. Heard she'd asked for ranger help."

"We've come," Barnes said. "This rustling up here, it something new?"

The storekeeper looked thoughtful. "Let me put it this way. Been awhile since there's been any to speak of, until now. Then Jane Covell got hit."

26

"Anybody else?"

"Most of the others are bigger than her. If they're missing cattle, they maybe don't know it yet."

"Where's the Covell place?"

"Let me sketch you out a map," the storekeeper said.

He went over to a counter, picked up a pencil, and tore off a piece from a roll of brown wrapping paper.

When he finished drawing, he came back and handed it to Barnes.

"Her house is about ten miles due south," he said. "Only one in the area. You won't miss it."

"Lady rancher," Barnes said. "Kind of unusual."

"Widow woman. Folks that know Covell like her. She's been running the spread since her husband died a couple years back. Heart attack."

"Interesting," Barnes said.

"If you're hungry, Rangers, I got foodstuffs here you can make a meal on."

Kenton spoke up then for the first time.

"We'll just take you up on that," he said.

The ranch yard was a utilitarian sprawl of small bunkhouse, sheds, and barn surrounding an unpainted board-and-batten dwelling.

"Ain't imposing," Kenton said.

"I've cowboyed for several like it," Barnes said. "Two-bit outfit, struggling to survive, by its look."

Kenton said, "That storekeep said there's bigger spreads around. Why'd the damn rustlers pick on this one?"

"Small crew, likely. The woman herself and a couple of riders, maybe."

At that moment the woman stepped out on the porch, a rifle in her hands. She was wearing riding pants and an open-necked blouse. Even at a distance Barnes could see she was young and pretty.

He called, "We're rangers. Heard we were needed."

"Ride in close," she called back, still keeping the rifle raised.

They moved in easily toward her, then halted.

"All right," she said. "I can see those stars now."

"We'll light then," Barnes said.

"Do so," she said. She stayed by the door.

They swung down and led their mounts to the nearby tie-rack.

"I'm Mrs. Covell," she said. "You'll have to excuse my being careful. I've been hit hard lately."

"We understand," Barnes said. What a fine-looking woman, he was thinking.

"Step inside. Are you hungry?"

"We ate at the Elgin store," Barnes said.

The inside of the place was almost as rough as the exterior. It was clean, and there were curtains on the windows and other signs of a woman's touch, but it was obvious that originally it had been a bachelor's abode.

She noted Barnes's survey of the sitting room and smiled a bit wryly, saying, "My late husband lived here alone for several years before I came. It's a man's place, and I've adapted to it, rather than trying to make major changes."

"No doubt running the ranch takes most of your interest," Barnes said.

"Yes, it does." She gestured to some homemade chairs, and they sat. "The cattle were stolen nearly two weeks ago. Thirty head. Four riders, by the hoofprints I saw."

"Did you track them far?"

"Tracks were a couple of days old when we discovered them. One of my two hired hands first noticed the stock missing from my south graze. No way we could catch up, and if we did, what could we do? My men are long-experienced cowhands, but not gunfighters. That's when I rode over to Sonoita, where there's a telephone, to call your headquarters."

"Best thing you could've done, lady," Kenton said. "Guns is something we know."

She gave him an odd look, then turned back to Barnes.

"Thirty head is a big loss on a spread this small," she said.

"Were they headed south?" Barnes said.

"Yes. And, as you may know, from here we're no more than thirty miles from the border. And once across it . . . well, I heard you rangers sometimes don't let the border stop you."

Kenton had been running his eyes appraisingly over her. It wasn't often he got to feast his eyes on a girl in tight range clothes. That she seemed unaware of her effect on him only served to increase his titillation. He was a man who had little regard for women but heavy lust.

Without taking his eyes from her, he now said, "Don't you worry none about us crossing that border. Not when it's going to help you if we do, miss."

"*Missus*," she said, abruptly aware of his leering scrutiny. She flushed, and dislike flared in her.

The cattle tracks were plain. There had been no rain to erase them. They followed a twisting trail of prior use.

"Pipeline to the border," Kenton said.

"Looks so."

They made camp as dusk caught them where they guessed was halfway. At first light they were up and moving again.

At midmorning they rode in sight of a town. It had a Mexican look about its few structures, but they had seen no border markings before they entered, and a sign on a small building read in English *Lochiel Restaurant, Good Food.*

"Lochiel," Kenton said. "I heard of the place."

"Yeah, me too," Barnes said. "Rumor is there's some small-time smuggling, one kind or another goes through here. Just far enough east to avoid the customs agents at Nogales."

"Rustling too, it appears."

"That we now know," Barnes said. "Try the restaurant?"

When Kenton didn't answer, he led the way. The place was empty.

A man came out of the kitchen as they entered. He was wearing a food-stained apron, and a nervous expression as he spotted the badges on their coats. He gave no greeting.

"Couple of coffees," Barnes said, slipping onto a stool at the counter.

The man went back into the kitchen, and Barnes could see him through the opening, lifting a coffeepot from a range.

At that moment he turned and met Barnes's eyes, then his own fell. Presently he came through the door and placed their cups on the counter.

He said, "Men, I ain't no information bureau."

"Did we ask?" Kenton said.

"Maybe I was mistook," the cook said.

"Since you brought it up," Kenton said, "maybe you weren't."

"Then I say it again."

"What you got against lawmen?" Kenton said.

"Nothing," the man said. "But I run a business here. And it don't help me none to be seen talking to men that wear badges."

"Well," Kenton said, "there ain't nobody looking now."

"My answer's still the same."

Kenton scowled.

Barnes saw the scowl and said, "Ease up, Jake."

Kenton ignored him and said to the owner, "Listen, you, a herd of cattle went through here a couple of weeks back. What ranches lie south of here?"

"A lot of them. Hell, all over Sonora. Anybody knows that."

"I'm going to ask you once more—in a nice way," Kenton said. "Where would be a place them cattle might have been headed?"

"I ain't a Mexican," the man said. "I ain't never been south of the border. But the nearest little town that the trail south goes through, I hear, is called Cruz. Ranch or two down there, I heard."

Barnes downed his coffee.

"Thanks," he said.

Kenton downed his. "We'll be coming through here on our way back," he said to the man behind the counter.

It sounded like a threat, the man thought, but he said nothing more as he watched them leave.

A couple of hours' ride took them to the town the restaurant owner had mentioned.

It wasn't much: a clutch of adobe dwellings and a few shops.

"We'd best take off these badges," Barnes said.

"Damned if I will," Kenton said. "I'm a ranger, and I want them to know it."

"We've got no legal authority down here."

"You think these *cholos* know that?"

"That'd be my guess."

"If they do or they don't, it makes no difference to me."

Barnes gave it some thought. "You may be right," he said finally.

Kenton made no reply.

"Cantina there," Barnes said.

They dismounted and entered.

Behind the bar was a short, young Mexican with a heavy black mustache. His dark eyes went from their faces to their nickeled stars, then back to their faces. The bar was empty.

Kenton asked, in English, "You got decent whiskey?"

"Of course."

"It better be," Kenton said.

The barkeep turned to Barnes, "And you, señor?"

"The same," Barnes said.

The barman set out glasses and poured.

Kenton tasted his drink. "Rotgut!"

"Is true of all whiskey, no?" the Mexican said.

Kenton tossed down the drink, not answering.

"Arizona Rangers, eh?"

"So you can read English, too," Kenton said.

The cantina door opened, and a tall gaunt native with Indian features staggered in.

"Get out!" the Mexican said.

Kenton's glance went to the Indian.

"Let him stay," he said.

"This is my cantina," the barman said.

"And this is my badge," Kenton said. "Let him stay. He looks like he could use another drink."

"He's had enough," the barman said.

Kenton said, "Hey, you! Come over and have a drink on us."

The Indian gave him a blank look.

Kenton raised his hand and flicked it toward himself.

The Indian understood then. He came jerkily toward him.

"Give him a drink of whatever he drinks," Kenton said.

The barman frowned, hesitated, then brought up a bottle of tequila and a glass and poured a shot.

The Indian grasped the glass, raised it with a shaking hand, and downed its contents.

Kenton watched his face, saw some of the agony subside.

He turned then to the Mexican and said, "We're trailing some cattle that was driven through here. What can you tell us about it?"

"Nothing," the Mexican said.

"I figured that," Kenton said. "Give my Indian friend here another tequila."

"You going to get him loose-mouthed?" the Mexican said. "You going to pump him for information?"

"Any objection?"

"I don't like it."

"Tough," Kenton said.

Barnes said suddenly. "He looks kind of familiar to me."

"He wasn't always a drunk," the Mexican said. "He and his cousins once had a little plot of ground they farmed down near Guerra. Raised enough food to feed themselves. Yaquis were farming farther south along the Yaqui River for centuries."

"So?" Kenton said.

"Couple years back the climate went bad on them. Lost their crops for two seasons. They tried to get some food from a mine company east of here and got shot up. This one escaped, wounded, but he's never been the same since."

"God!" Barnes said.

Kenton and the barman both looked at him.

"What's that mean?" Kenton said.

Barnes just shook his head, giving no answer.

Kenton turned to the Yaqui, and said in his border Spanish, "You talk to me, I buy you drinks."

The Yaqui was beginning to shake again. He nodded eagerly.

"Serve him," Kenton said to the barman.

The Mexican poured a double shot of tequila.

The Yaqui grabbed and drank it. He seemed to become alert.

He said, in broken English, "I hear what you say to Enrique here about the cattle. I see them go by down trail. Maybe go to Cocóspera. Big ranch, like them cattle."

"Cocóspera, huh?" Kenton said.

"I told you," the Yaqui said. "You buy me bottle tequila now?"

"Hell, no!" Kenton said. He turned away and started for the door.

Barnes fished some money out of his pocket, gestured to the tequila bottle, and said to the bar man, "Let him have what's left."

"It will cost you."

"I'm paying."

The Mexican reached out and took the American coins from his hand.

Barnes took a long last look at the Yaqui. He dropped a hand on his shoulder as he passed him, following Kenton out.

They mounted and rode out of town before Kenton spoke.

"What the hell was that Yaqui to you?"

Barnes said regretfully, "It was me who shot up him and those others when they raided for food at the mine."

The trail skirted a low range of mountains to the west. Near nightfall they approached an intersection with a dirt road heading southwest that showed occasional use.

There was a crudely lettered wood sign facing them. An arrow pointing easterly was labeled CANANEA. An opposite one was lettered MAGDALENA. Neither gave the distance.

"That mine we guarded was over Cananea way," Barnes said.

"I never knew why you quit," Kenton said.

Barnes didn't answer him.

That was a way they frequently conversed, neither replying to the other if he didn't feel like it. Part of their strange relationship, Barnes thought. A way of keeping distance between them, even as they worked together.

"We should have talked a little longer to the Yaqui," Barnes said.

"I never could stand a drunken Indian," Kenton said.

They made camp then, neither saying any more.

In the morning, as soon as they had saddled up, Kenton led the way south.

Barnes made no comment. It would have been his choice of direction likewise.

A dozen miles or so later they met a squad of mounted Rurales.

The sergeant leading them halted and raised his palm in command for Kenton and Barnes to stop.

He studied the stars they wore, then spoke. "Gringo rangers, eh? Where do you go? And what do you do this far south of the border, in my country? I am Sergeant Soto asking."

"We're looking for American rustlers of American cattle," Barnes said. "Four of them. Have you seen anyone who might be those men?"

"Perhaps," the sergeant said. "What is it worth to you to know?"

"We rangers and you Rurales have cooperated before," Barnes said.

"Possibly so," the Rurale chief said. "But I, personally, have not. I, personally, do not like you gringo lawmen in my country, intruding."

"We do not mean to intrude," Barnes said. "But as a lawman yourself, aren't you interested in the apprehension of rustlers?"

"Rustlers of American cattle? No, not particularly. At the present I am interested in catching marauding bands of rebellious Yaquis who are fighting against the legitimate government of Mexico."

Barnes was silent.

But Kenton said, "Looking for Yaquis, huh?"

"You know something?" the Rurale said. "Then maybe we can trade information."

"There is said to be a band of them close by, in a place called Guerra. Only a few more miles in the direction you're going."

The *Rurale* looked thoughtful. "We will continue on to there, then. Myself and my men are seldom sent this far north, and this is news."

"Those, though, are peaceful Yaquis," Barnes said.

The *jefe* stared at him. "Amigo, there are no peaceful Yaquis. And in appreciation of what your *compadre* has told me, I will tell you we encountered four gringo riders, such as you have asked about. A few kilómetros back. In Co-cóspera."

He paused, then said, "They were drunk, and spending well in the cantina there. So I left them alone, to please the owner." His voice hardened. "But you want them, you take them alive, understand? Every time a gringo is killed down here, your *maldito* government blames my country for it. You kill, we get the blame. So, you kill, we lock you up in a *juzgado* to rot."

He rode past them then, leading his squad away.

Barnes said angrily, "You shouldn't have told him about the Yaquis."

"It got us news about the rustlers," Kenton said. "Blowing the money they got from some Mex rancher for the cattle they stole."

"That Rurale chief is on a Yaqui hunt," Barnes said. "He'll kill them when he gets to Guerra."

Kenton shrugged. "Why do you side with Yaquis?"

"You want to know? I'll tell you why. After I shot up those poor bastards at the mine, I read all I could find about their treatment by the Spanish and, later, the Mexican government."

"They've always been rebels," Kenton said, "the way I hear it."

"They've always had reason to be. Their homeland was the fertile agricultural land along the Yaqui River. And the government has never stopped trying to cheat them out of it."

Kenton listened in silence. Finally he said, "I didn't know that." There was no expression in his voice.

Barnes studied his face, and there was no expression there either. If Kenton felt regret, he didn't show it.

Instead, he led off down the road toward Magdalena.

Twelve miles later they came to the little town of Cocóspera.

Barnes said, "That Rurale could've been lying about gringos here."

"I see only one cantina. It won't take long to find out."

"What we want to do first," Barnes said, "is find out where they sold the cattle." He was taking off the ranger star he had pinned on when talking to the Rurales.

Kenton did likewise.

They dismounted in front of the nearest cantina.

Inside was a Mexican bartender, idly watching them as they entered.

In one rear corner, at a table, were seated three gringos in range clothes. They looked drunk.

Another moved aside from the open doorway as Kenton pushed by.

Barnes, just behind, noted this, and wondered if the man had been watching their approach. He remained by the door as Kenton and Barnes moved toward the bar.

The bartender said, "Whiskey?"

"How'd you know?" Kenton said.

The bartender did not smile. He had a tired expression on his face. "I learn from these others what gringos like," he said.

"They good spenders?" Kenton said.

"Very good," the Mexican said.

"Then you should be looking happier than you do," Kenton said.

"Money isn't everything," the Mexican said. "They been *borracho* now for two, three days. It can wear on a man."

"We may have a word with them," Barnes said. "We may ask them to leave."

"That would be appreciated," the bartender said.

The one by the door crossed unsteadily to those at the table.

He did not look at the rangers as he passed.

"Is there a ranch around here where a rider might get a job?" Barnes said.

"There are a few."

"Which is the most likely to hire us two *vaqueros*?" Kenton said.

"You are cowboys, señor?"

"What do we look like?"

The Mexican hesitated. "I saw you, through the window, take off your badges, señor."

"The drunk in the doorway," Barnes said, "did he see that, too?"

"He is not yet *blind* drunk," the Mexican said.

The rangers tossed down their drinks.

The barkeep said, "I could not tell what kind of badges you wore."

Kenton took his from a pocket and held it so it could be read.

"Ah," the Mexican said. "*Rangeros*."

Kenton said to Barnes, "It's time we acted."

"Lead on," Barnes said.

They drew their guns and went toward the table where the four drunk gringos were talking among themselves.

At their approach, the four turned to look and one of them, who seemed even more drunk than the rest, called out, "Hey, amigos!"

He was either too drunk to notice or chose to ignore their drawn weapons.

As far as Barnes could see, they all had holstered guns.

"Have a drink, *amigos*."

"We'd rather have a talk," Barnes said.

He and Kenton had taken stances several feet apart.

"Talk then."

"Where did you sell the cattle?" Kenton said.

"What cattle?"

"Thirty head you rustled off the Covell ranch up Elgin way."

"You must have us mistook for somebody else," the spokesman drunk said.

The one who had been at the doorway seemed to remember then what he had seen. He said, "I think maybe these are rangers."

"Rangers?" the spokesman said.

And at that moment one of them, who was seated across the table, clumsily drew a gun from beneath it, striking the edge as he did so.

He got no further with it, as Kenton drew and fired. Blood spurted from the man's throat.

None of the others moved.

But Kenton kept shooting, fast, all around the table.

Barnes reached for his own gun. But there was no need for it. All four of the rustlers were dead.

Barnes stared from one to the other. There was no movement.

He said then, "What did you gain by that?"

Kenton said, "Four dead bastards that won't steal any more cattle."

"And the cattle they stole? You just ruined the chance to learn where they sold them."

"Such things happen. One of them drew first."

"Covell won't be satisfied with this. Ryerson won't either. And that *Rurale* chief warned us!"

Kenton gave him a stare. "Listen, I'm a ranger because I like the kind of work it lets me do. But if Ryerson doesn't like it, he can end my enlistment anytime."

"Man," Barnes said, "you got to be kill-crazy!"

"That's what they sent me to Cuba to do," Kenton said, then paused. "And I found I liked it."

"God!"

"That surprise you?"

Barnes did not answer at once. Then he said, "To hear you say it, yes. . . . But I've had some wonder."

Kenton's face hardened. "Now you know."

Barnes was silent.

Kenton's eyes were on him, watching as Barnes stared again at the scattered bodies. "You want to know how it came about?"

Without looking at him, Barnes said, "There were a lot of men went to fight in Cuba. I never before heard one say he liked the killing he did."

"You want to hear what made it happen to me?"

Barnes said nothing, but he waited.

Kenton said, "It happened at Las Guásimas. You know about Guásimas?"

"I know what I read in the newspapers at the time."

"Then you know it happened several days before the charge up San Juan Hill. I was hit at Guásimas, so I missed the Hill."

"Bad wounded?"

"Bad enough. I took three Mauser bullets from a Spanish rear guard waiting for us. They were up on a ridge, and knew we were coming. Guásimas was a crossroads in the middle of a jungle so thick we didn't even see them at first. It was an ambush, pure and simple, but I never blamed our officers.

"We crawled around in that jungle growth until we found positions to spot our attackers, and it was sniper fire between their Mauser rifles and our Krags.

"The battle went on like that for near three hours. I was hit once early on, and then twice more, but that didn't take me out of action. It just made me mad. I began to find targets, here and there, and for a spell I had the best hunting of my life. I kept making hits. I figured I shot a dozen of the bastards, and I loved it each time I did. Maybe because I was in pain myself.

"Let me tell you, despite my hurting, those were the most gratifying moments of my life."

Kenton paused, then said, "And every time I've triggered a round into an outlaw I get that same feeling, something I get in no other way. It's like I was lying there wounded in that jungle and doing it all over again."

It was as strange a story as Barnes had ever heard. It answered a question that had long been on his mind.

But the answer didn't make him feel any better.

CHAPTER 5

THE MEXICAN BARTENDER came over to them, his eyes fixed on the four dead men.

He could hear Kenton talking, but seemed to be paying no attention to what he said. When Kenton was finished, the bartender said, "You may be in much trouble, *amigos*. Here in Sonora, there is a law against murder."

"Murder?" Kenton said. "These are *ladrónes* who stole American cattle to sell down here. And we are rangers sent to arrest them."

"To arrest, that is acceptable," the Mexican said. "But to kill like this, that may not be."

"You saw them resist arrest," Kenton said.

"I did?"

Kenton gave him a hard look. "Yes," he said. "You saw one of them pull a gun on me."

The Mexican met his look for a while. Then his eyes fell, and he said, "Maybe I did see that."

"That's better," Kenton said.

His patronizing tone angered the barman. "But only because they been gringo. You understand? If they been Mexican, I don't see nothing."

"Good enough," Kenton said.

The killing still seemed to bother the barkeep.

He said, "How you know, they been rustlers? You don't even ask."

Kenton didn't answer. Instead he said, "What's the biggest ranch around here?"

"That of Don Jorge Ribera. Maybe these men been some he hired lately. He raise many cattle."

"Buys some that are stolen too, maybe," Kenton said. "Stolen from above the border."

"No, señor, not Don Jorge. I do not believe that."

Barnes said, "Have you got a lawman in this town?"

"Only sometimes the Rurales. It happens they passed through here before you came."

"When will they be back?" Barnes said.

"Who knows?" the barman said. "Don Jorge must be told what you did here. Like I say, these maybe some new men he hire."

"We'll tell him," Barnes said.

Kenton gave him an angry look. "You damn fool, we got to get out of here. Did you forget what that Rurale sergeant said about jailing us to rot?"

"We can't just run," Barnes said. "We've got to explain what happened."

"Listen, I spent a month in one of these Mex jails once," Kenton said. "I ain't about to let it happen again."

It had been only four miles to the place called Guerra, soon reached by the Rurales after meeting the two gringo rangers.

Sergeant Soto did not like the idea of gringo lawmen entering places in his jurisdiction. They were arrogant bastards, he thought. But when he quickly reached the cultivated fields and noted the Yaqui type *jacales* scattered about, some of his animosity waned. The one ranger had given him a good tip, he had to admit.

"Ready your weapons!" he commanded

His second in command, the one called Toriano, said then, "I see no targets, *jefe*."

"No targets?"

"There are no Yaquis working in the fields."

Soto's eyes studied the cultivated plots. "So!" he said. "The Yaquis are perhaps loafing in their *jacales,* as all Indians like to do. But we will approach them cautiously."

* * *

Barnes said to the Mexican bartender, "Where is the ranch of this Don Jorge Ribera?"

"If you rode in from the east, you passed the road that leads southward to his hacienda," the barkeep said. "It is maybe six or eight miles to where that turnoff is."

"Let's go!" Barnes said to Kenton.

Kenton started to object, then nodded.

Barnes understood the change. Kenton would be thinking about the main road being the one leading back to the border. The argument would come later when they reached the intersection with the ranch road.

He led the way outside.

They mounted without another word and rode off eastward. The silence continued between them. Barnes was seething inwardly at the turn their mission had taken. That goddamned Kenton was too fast with his gun—too fast and too accurate. When he shot, he left no wounded.

Such shooting had to be part luck, he thought. But part only. The bastard had a rare native ability as a marksman. An ability that led to trouble. Trouble that Barnes wondered how they would get out of.

Were the four men lying dead back there in the cantina the rustlers they had been seeking? Or, as the barman stated, had they been innocent riders of the local *hacendado*?

At that moment he had no way of knowing. But there was one thing he did know: When, or if, they got back across the border, he was shedding himself of his obstreperous partner.

His thoughts were interrupted some time later.

"Dust up ahead. And coming this way," Kenton said. He was already turning north off the road and into the adjoining brush. He said, "Lay low until we see who's kicking it up."

Barnes followed him until they were hid.

*　　*　　*

There were a half dozen armed Yaquis in the hastily formed band following the returning Rurale squad who had set fire to their farm *jacales* after finding they had gone into hiding.

The Yaquis had been alerted by a chance sighting of their approach and had remained hidden while they watched their shelters being destroyed. But once the Rurales withdrew and the Yaquis returned to survey their bitter loss, their fighting blood boiled to a demand for vengeance.

They quickly formed under a leader, Husakamea, and trailed the hated police. They kept on the flanks, slipping with Yaqui adeptness through the heavy brush that screened any rising of dust.

Husakamea was wise enough not to pick a fight on the open road. His plan, as they drew within firing range, was to open sniper fire.

He was about to give the order when the Rurales halted, then turned aside to the north and disappeared into the brush themselves.

It was Toriano, the Rurales' best tracker, who had seen the prints that caused Sergeant Soto to halt.

"See there, *jefe*," Toriano said. "Those are tracks just made by a pair of riders. Made only minutes ago. And where I noticed dust just then. Would you say they are those of riders who might be wishing to avoid us?"

"We have no need to hurry," Soto said. "We will follow to see who they are."

Hidden in the brush, only yards away, Barnes glimpsed the halted squad as they changed direction.

"It's the Rurales," he said. "Our best bet is to wait and explain what happened in Cocóspera."

"Like hell!" Kenton said. "I ain't risking doing time in one of their stinking jails. I told you that."

Barnes was ready to argue.

But a moment later Kenton was gone.

Barnes cursed under his breath. But Kenton's flight made its impression. Those Mexican jails, others had told him, were usually hellholes. And if Kenton, who had experience in one of them, was ready to run to avoid a second experience . . .

An instant later Barnes was following at Kenton's heels. He was still cursing, at himself or Kenton or both, he wasn't sure which. Because the thought was with him now that the chances of escaping the Rurale squad were considerably less than even. Their mounts had been ridden for days now, without livery care or feed. He expected those of the Rurales had been better treated.

They moved through the brush at a fast walk, and he assumed the Rurales were doing likewise. But sooner or later they would break out into scantier growth, and in more open country they would almost certainly be overtaken.

That would mean a standoff, the two of them against the Rurale sergeant and his six-man squad.

Not even Kenton's fast gun could even up odds like those.

Without hope now, he continued to blindly follow Kenton's lead.

When the gunfire broke loose behind him he instinctively leaned forward, low over his horse's neck, expecting the bullets to sing by if he was lucky, to hit him if he wasn't.

Neither happened.

Just ahead, Kenton was coming to a halt.

As Barnes joined him, they sat listening to the weapon fire.

Kenton said, "Hell, that's two-sided firing."

"How can you tell?"

"Battle fire," Kenton said. "Once you've heard it, you never forget it. Something about the spacing."

"One is the Rurales. Who's the other?"

"That I can't say," Kenton said. "But it's a break for us. Let's ride!"

He took off then, and presently they broke out into sparse country again. The land here sloped upward toward a nearby range of hills.

They climbed a short distance, then Kenton stopped once to look back. They could still hear the shooting, although sporadic, and they could see a faint rising of gunsmoke above where it was taking place. But the participants were hidden by the scrub.

"Whoever it was, they done us a favor," Kenton said. "It gave us a breather."

"I'm wondering who it was," Barnes said.

"Not likely we'll ever know," Kenton said. "Somebody who don't like Rurales, that's for sure."

The casualties were high.

The element of surprise had been with the Yaquis, though they were not the best of shots. But they had knocked one Rurale out of his saddle in the initial attack.

The Rurales dismounted, dove for cover, then gave retaliatory fire as the Indians closed in on their diminished targets.

One Yaqui fell before they went prone to crawl almost silently, searching out their foes.

Suddenly they were close enough that each side was again revealed to the other.

In the exchange, both sides scored again, though misses were many. But the Rurales were the better marksmen. They lost another man, but made two more hits.

There were now three Yaquis alive against seven Rurales,

counting Sergeant Soto and two who were seriously wounded.

The Indians withdrew, dragging their dead with them.

It was then that Sergeant Soto discovered he had taken a bullet in his left arm, and it was bleeding badly.

Toriano said, "We have badly wounded men, I think, *jefe.* Including yourself. Wounds that need attention. Perhaps in Cocóspera?"

"We will start to withdraw," Soto said. "What we do then depends on these devil Yaquis."

The Yaqui leader was enraged by his losses, yet he still lusted for revenge for the burning of the Yaqui houses.

He hated whites, a race in which he classified Mexicans as well as the Spanish who had victimized his forebears. Nothing changes, he thought bitterly. Hundreds of years, and nothing changes. They are all against us Yaquis.

Even now Mexican government officials were abducting Yaqui men, women and children to sell as slaves to the wealthy hemp farmers in the far-off Yucatan. It was a double-edged sword they swung at his people, because the Mexicans then took over the lands from which the Yaquis had been removed.

It was one of his men who noticed the tracks left by the horses of Barnes and Kenton. The Yaqui leader knew he would suffer further losses if he renewed his attack on the Rurales, now that the element of surprise was gone. Still he was aroused, and suddenly, driven by a smoldering emotional need, he said, "We will follow the trail of the two. They are likely whites—they have left the prints of shod hoofs."

"But our dead?" one of his men said.

"We will return for them later," Husakamea replied, and began following the tracks. The other two fell in behind.

*   *   *

Kenton stopped again as they climbed toward a high pass in the hill range. The way was steep enough that the horses needed respite.

It was then they saw the riders appear out of the brush.

Barnes studied them and said, "Indians or Mexican. But not in the clothes of Rurales."

"There's no trail except the one we're leaving. Whoever they are, they're interested in us."

"Could be so," Barnes said.

"There's no cover here," Kenton said. "There's three to our two. No place for a close-up battle."

"We don't know if they're against us," Barnes said.

Kenton didn't seem to hear. He said, "You're a better shot with a rifle at distance. They get into range, try your luck."

"Dammit! Will you listen? They may not mean us harm."

"Yeah, maybe," Kenton said. "Well, let's ride on. If they gain on us, and it comes to trouble, we're better off in the hills."

"All right. Move out."

They resumed their climb.

Eventually they entered the shallow pass.

At last look, the three riders had gained considerably.

"We may have a showdown here in the hills," Kenton said.

Barnes was silent. His own curiosity was growing. At first he had thought the riders might turn aside as they reached the climb, but it was apparent now this was not going to happen.

He said, then, "Pick a spot for a defense."

Kenton had been looking at the far end of the pass. He said, "Ahead there, where the gap seems to end. Looks like some outthrusts of shale. Might do for a breastwork."

They headed toward it.

Reaching it, Kenton said, "Good enough."

The west side of the rocks appeared to be the most protected, and they took up positions there. They kept hidden except to peer briefly through a cleft in the shale at the oncoming riders.

They were nearing effective rifle range, but Barnes did not sight his weapon.

"What's wrong?" Kenton said.

"Waiting to see if they're friend or foe," Barnes said.

"Goddammit, they're enemy!"

"You don't know that."

"I'm guessing," Kenton said, raising his rifle.

Barnes reached over and shoved the barrel upward as Kenton fired.

"The riders halted.

"You goddam fool!" Kenton said. "I could have picked off one, maybe two."

"They're close enough that I can tell they're Yaqui. They're wearing moccasins."

"When they wear moccasins in this day and age, it must mean they're on the warpath," Kenton said.

"Their battle is against the Mexican officials."

"You don't ever know how an Indian's mind will work if he's stirred up about something."

"Let me parley with them and find out," Barnes said.

"Look. You step out there, I'm going to be left one against three of the bastards."

Barnes ignored him. He slipped off his neckerchief, tied it to his rifle barrel, and raised it so the riders could see it.

When no fire came, he cautiously arose and called, in Spanish, "I wish to talk, *amigos*."

His voice must have reached them, because one, presumably the leader, gestured with his arm for Barnes to come forward.

"You're a fool," Kenton said. But he made no move to hold him back as Barnes mounted his horse and rode out from the cover.

It was a couple of hundred yards to where the riders

sat their saddles, waiting. Two of them held rifles pointed generally in Kenton's direction. The leader had his hands resting on the horn of his saddle.

"You are Yaquis?" Barnes called as he neared them.

The leader called back, "We are Yaquis!" He said it proudly, with defiance.

And with threat, Barnes thought. He was beginning to feel this could be a mistake.

"I am a friend of the Yaquis. I sympathize with your problems."

"Come closer, friend of the Yaquis," the leader said. "We will talk about this."

When Barnes was ten yards away, the leader said, "So you are gringo. But gringos, like Mexicans, have killed many Yaquis in their time."

"I am your friend," Barnes said again.

The Yaqui's face had been expressionless. But now, suddenly, it hardened. "You!" he said.

"Me?"

The Yaqui said to his men, "Shoot this one if he moves."

The two turned their weapons to cover Barnes.

"So, you are our friend?" the leader said. "I remember you from the time, it makes two, three years now."

"We have met?" Barnes said.

"Oh, yes, we have met, gringo friend of the Yaquis. I was close enough to see well your face when you put a bullet in me and in the others with me."

Yes, Barnes thought, it was a mistake to ask for this parley.

"You remember that time, gringo? At the mine near Cananea?"

He remembered, but he did not recognize the Yaqui's face. Especially now. With the Yaqui weapons pointed at him.

I should have listened to Kenton, he thought.

One of the Yaquis said to the leader, "I would take pleasure in being the one to shoot him."

"Not yet," the leader said. And then to Barnes, "Dismount, friend of the Yaquis. But drop your weapons first."

With two rifle muzzles fixed on him, Barnes reluctantly complied.

As his boots touched the ground, he turned his eyes toward the shale rampart. Kenton would be watching, he thought. Kenton would be cursing him for being a damn fool.

The Yaqui leader saw his glance and said, "I want your amigo to watch what we do to you next."

Hearing those words, Barnes had a moment of regret that he'd not made a dash for it, even though the Yaqui weapons would have meant quick, sure death.

That would have been better than what might lie ahead. For all of his sympathy with the Yaqui cause, he was well aware of the Indian ways of treating those they considered enemies.

He looked again at where Kenton was hidden. At best, Kenton could only fire a chancy shot, which would probably be ineffective in halting the Yaqui's actions.

"Tie his hands and feet," the leader said, drawing a revolver from his belt. He tossed a couple of thongs nearby.

The other two put down their rifles and grabbed Barnes and threw him to the ground.

As one reached for the thongs, Barnes kicked out with both feet, sending him sprawling.

The other threw his weight onto Barnes, trying to hold him down. But Barnes got an arm loose and drove his fist against his jaw, stunning him.

The leader was pointing his gun at the struggling pair, not firing for fear of hitting his confederate.

And at that moment, the leader heard the sound of pounding hoofs racing toward him. He looked up and saw the other white, low in the saddle, pistol in hand, coming into firing range.

The Yaqui leader raised his gun to exchange shots with Kenton. He missed, but Kenton didn't.

With one Yaqui stunned by his driving fist, Barnes tore free and dove for one of their rifles just as the other Yaqui did. They collided, then fought to grasp the gun.

Barnes clutched the stock as the Yaqui grabbed the barrel. Barnes's finger sought the trigger and pressed it, even as he was losing his grip.

He felt the heat of the burning powder, the exploding blast, and the thrust away of the Yaqui's body as the bullet smashed through his chest bones.

Kenton was close now and fired again as the last Yaqui reached for the other rifle. Kenton's bullet put a stop to that.

They unsaddled the Yaquis' horses, turned them free, and rode away from the bodies.

They rode for a long time in silence.

It was Barnes who finally spoke.

"You saved my life again," he said. "And from torture. That Yaqui had a knife ready to carve my carcass."

Kenton said, "How the hell could you have had any sympathy for a bastard like that?"

Barnes did not answer at once. He was thinking it over. How could he?

"Well?" Kenton said.

Still bothered by having had to kill, Barnes said, "The leader had his reason. He was one of those I shot when they raided for food at Cananea."

"Listen, forget all that," Kenton said. "War is a here-and-now thing. And this was a small war. Don't you understand? War is when you decide who your enemy of the moment is, and you go all out to kill him. Otherwise you die yourself." He paused, then said, "If you're a ranger, outlaws anywhere are your enemies."

CHAPTER 6

THEY REPORTED IN to headquarters at Douglas, a two-room adobe with an office in front, tack room in back, and a corral for horses behind it.

Captain Ryerson was waiting for them. He did not greet them warmly.

"Before you make your report," he said, his voice hard, "let me tell you Colonel Kosterlitzky, down in Magdalena, contacted me by phone. I have his description of what happened, as given him by a squad of his Rurales. To say he is irate is to put it mildly. He threatens to end our unofficial working agreement of cooperation against outlaw border jumpers from either nation."

The two rangers were silent.

"Do you know what that means? It means no more easy access into Mexico in pursuit of a criminal on the run. It's the biggest blow we could have against our success in cleaning up outlawry in Arizona—which is what the hell we were formed to do."

Kenton said, "Things just kind of went wrong for us down there, Cap."

"You botched your mission," Ryerson said.

"We got the rustlers we went after, Cap."

"You killed them," Ryerson said, "before you could find out from them where they sold the cattle."

Barnes said, "We had a lead to investigate. But we had to run to keep from being jailed by a gringo-hating Rurale sergeant."

"Mostly they cooperate," Ryerson said.

"Not this one," Kenton said. "He had already made his threat."

"The *cantinero* who reported the shooting told Kosterlitzky only one of you triggered the shots that killed. Which one of you?"

There was a short silence, then Kenton said, "I did. And glad of it."

"I guessed. You're too trigger-happy, Kenton."

"You ain't going to clean up Arizona with a force of Sunday-school teachers, Cap."

"We don't want any," Ryerson said. "We want hard men who can get the job done. Some of you bring down criticism by the press and by the governor's political opponents, but I ignore that. What I do object to, is when harsh treatment defeats getting the job done right. As in this case."

Kenton said, "What happened wasn't intentional on my part. As to how I think about what we're given to do, I feel we ain't a police force. We're an army, small as it is, and an army's job is to kill the enemy. This star on my chest gives me that permit, just as my soldier uniform did in Cuba."

Listening to this, Barnes was weighing in his own mind how to present a request for severance from this partner without offending him. God, he owed his life, two or three times over, to Kenton!

While he hesitated, the opportunity seemed to pass, because Ryerson said, "Kosterlitzky admitted that the four you killed had a reputation for bringing down cattle to sell at bargain prices." He paused. "So you did accomplish something."

"Nothing said about who bought them?" Barnes said.

"I asked, of course. But some of those Mexican ranchers carry political clout down there. All I got was a statement that it would be investigated. I won't be holding my breath."

"So Jane Covell is out the price of thirty head," Barnes said.

"At least she won't be rustled by the same thieves again, Cap," Kenton said.

"I've taken that into consideration, so you get another chance," the captain said to Kenton, "and I'm keeping Barnes with you."

"Why?" Barnes said.

"Maybe he'll learn a little moderation from you," Ryerson replied.

Barnes knew Kenton better than that.

The chance that Ryerson was giving them sure as hell wasn't a reward, Barnes was thinking. As he had it figured, it was more like a punishment.

Ryerson told them about two bandits, thought to be Mexican nationals, who had begun to appear in a spree of stage, railroad, and bank robberies all over the Territory. Rangers had gone out to hunt them, but so far had had no luck.

Meanwhile they had been reported in Globe, Safford, Willcox, Benson, and a half dozen other places.

You could discount most of the sightings, Barnes knew. People had a way of mistaking identities in these things, particularly in cases involving Mexicans.

There had been credible reports, though, from three crime scenes in recent weeks. One was an attempted rail holdup at San Simón while the train was stopped; a guard was badly wounded when he refused to give in to the demands of the robber pair. The shooting attracted the attention of several witnesses, who described the fleeing criminals and their mounts.

Another was the halting of a stage outside Casa Grande. Halted by the killing of the driver and the shotgun messenger. Four passengers had been robbed of a total of a couple of hundred dollars, but let live. They later vouched for the resemblance of the killers to wanted dodgers they were shown.

The bandits were dealing death and wounds, it appeared, but gaining little financially.

They did a little better at a bank at Greaterville where they got away with five hundred dollars or thereabouts, but fled the town pursued by a townsmen posse who lost them shortly afterward.

This had been the last reported sighting, wired to Ryerson the day before. The ranger captain continued, "Get to Greaterville. Start your search from there."

"A long ride," Kenton said.

"Take the train up to Pantano; put your horses in a stock car. That's the closest spot to unload. Greaterville's maybe twenty miles south. Take fresh mounts from our cavvy. And I want you on the morning train."

For a moment Kenton looked like he was about to object. He and Barnes were plenty trail weary.

But he ended up saying only, "Okay, Cap. It's a war, ain't it?"

"That it is," Ryerson said.

The posse members at Greaterville had little to say to the newly arrived pair of rangers.

As happened a lot of places nowadays when rangers were sent in to solve problems locals couldn't handle themselves, there was an element of resentment, although usually tempered by relief.

Those men who briefed Barnes and Kenton on their own failure couldn't contribute much except "Them bastard Mexes is likely hiding out awhile up in the Santa Ritas behind us here. But, hell, ain't none of us mountain trackers."

One of the posse riders did take the rangers out as far as they had followed the bandits three days before. He left them then, with a "Good luck!" thrown over his shoulder.

After a moderate search they found the trail sign left by the criminals, although it soon led them into rougher country.

Ahead, in the distance, they could see a peak rising above the mountainous terrain and its growth of fir and pine.

Barnes unfolded a map Ryerson had given him. He said, "Mount Wrightson, if this map isn't lying."

Kenton gave him a glance, then said, "Ain't likely those *cholos* got a map. They could get themselves lost and us too."

But they soon began to come upon evidence of rest stops, and after the first day's ride, a campsite.

"Don't appear they're in much of a hurry," Barnes said.

"Probably guessed they shook the posse," Kenton said. "There was a high spot behind us where they could have seen a long ways down their backtrail."

"We may catch up soon, then."

"Sooner the better," Kenton said.

"Captain would be damn glad to see us bring them in," Barnes said.

Kenton made no reply.

Later, though, he said, "Just like a couple of Mexicans, ain't it? They been working hard at what they do, but give them a chance to rest up, and they'll take full advantage of it."

"Another way to figure it," Barnes said, "is that when they come out of these mountains, and if they intend to maybe go back to Mexico, they may figure there'll be law waiting for them along the border for a while."

"You can't tell how a Mexican thinks," Kenton said.

Another day of riding, and the fugitives' trail sign showed for certain that they were lazying along.

And on the following morning, Barnes said, "We'll be closing in on them today."

"My guess, too."

They came to a place of rock and hard soil and no prints to see, although there was a faintly used existing trail.

But a short ways on it forked widely, one prong south-easterly, one toward the southwest. As far as they could see, the hard terrain carried no vestige of the quarry's trail.

"It looks like we split here," Kenton said.

"For how far?" Barnes said.

"Till we come to the bastards' tracks again."

"May be a wide split before we do," Barnes said.

"Soon as one of us hits onto something, fire a weapon. Gun sound in this kind of country will carry a lot of miles."

Barnes looked dubious. "Maybe."

"You got a better idea?" Kenton said.

"Reckon not."

Without another word, Kenton took the southeast fork.

Barnes hesitated until Kenton was almost out of sight. Then he frowned and took the other.

Word of the Greaterville bank robbery had reached the sheriff at Nogales. His name was Robert Castillo, and he was one of the many peace officers in the Territory who held a strong resentment against the ranger enforcement body that roamed freely into their jurisdictions to make arrests of their own.

Like others, he felt he was capable of administering the law in Santa Cruz County. Who needed an elite company of arrogant gunslingers to do the job?

When he learned that two of Ryerson's men had been sent out on the case, he had a sudden urge to involve himself on a search of his own.

And when a teamster down from Greaterville told him the bandits had disappeared into the Santa Ritas, he made his decision. This was a mountain range with which he had some familiarity from other manhunts.

He immediately saddled up, took along provisions to last him a few days, and headed north toward the mountains.

He was forty years old, and had been a lawman half his life, sheriff for nearly one term. Soon he would be coming up for reelection. In his mind was the thought that beating out a team of rangers could be a great asset toward a successful campaign.

Being of Mexican-American descent, he needed every asset he could muster. His first campaign for office had been a close one.

He entered the long and narrow mountain range from the south, where there were still active gold and silver mines among the vestiges of those that had been worked a century or more before by the Spaniards. This strategy would increase his chance of finding the fugitives, if they were heading this far south.

There was always a possibility, too, that some isolated mining man farther north had sighted the bandit pair.

He skirted the eastern side of the Wrightson peak, moving slow, his eyes roving the terrain unceasingly.

He was high on a north slope when he looked east and saw a scene that halted him.

Barnes had gone along the southwest fork, which now twisted due south through a series of rock outcroppings, for only a couple of miles when he heard sound of a rifle shot from Kenton's direction.

He immediately turned off the trail and cut through the timber toward the shot. The ground here sloped downward, ending at a steep bluff that gave view of a clearing some four hundred yards below.

Kenton was down there.

He was on foot, facing two dark-skinned men, with his rifle pointed at them. The two were dismounted, but the weapons of the pair were lying on the ground where they had dropped them.

They appeared to be staring at Kenton, and neither was making the slightest move.

Their horses were tethered a short distance away, unsaddled. Kenton's was hidden somewhere in the timber behind him. It was obvious to Barnes that Kenton had sneaked up on the unsuspecting pair.

Words were shouted across the thirty yards separating Kenton from the outlaws.

Barnes could faintly hear the sound, but could not distinguish the words at that distance. He judged by the gestures of the Mexicans that they were remonstrating with something Kenton had said.

Kenton listened, silent and rocklike.

One of them spoke again, and pointed toward one of the horses.

This time Kenton nodded, and the man moved to the mount, fumbled in a saddlebag, and withdrew a sack, the kind that banks use for transporting money. He tossed it to land several feet in front of him.

Stupid, Barnes thought as he watched. They were still carrying the currency in the sack they had stolen it in.

Stupid and careless—two things an outlaw should never be when confronted by Kenton.

And at that moment he sensed what was coming, and shouted, loud as he could, a protest.

He was too late.

His cry was drowned out by the two shots fired point blank by Kenton.

The two Mexicans fell and did not move.

From a quarter mile south, Sheriff Robert Castillo saw it all happen. Beset by raging emotions, he kicked his horse into a trot toward the scene.

Made reckless by anger, Barnes was already on his way, risking his mount on the sharp descent from the bluff. This time, Kenton had gone too far.

He burst into the clearing to see Kenton calmly waiting for him.

"Heard you coming," Kenton said.

"You cold-blooded bastard!"

"They deserved it," Kenton said. "Shot up a railroad express guard. Killed a stage driver and his shotgun messenger. Remember?"

"That don't give you the right to execute them without a trial!"

"Quick justice is what will win this war we're fighting," Kenton said.

Barnes, nerves jumping at the atrocity, slipped from his saddle to go over to where the two Mexicans lay. He bent over each one checking for life.

He stood up and said dully, "Both dead."

"Hell," Kenton said, "at thirty yards, how could I miss?"

"God!" Barnes said. "You're not human."

"I figure," Kenton said, "you got to do what has to be done."

"There was no call for it here."

"If you had seen it all," Kenton said, "you'd have seen one of them try to bribe me with that money." He nodded at the sack still lying on the ground.

"I saw it all," Barnes said. "Is an attempted bribe all it takes to make you kill?"

"No," Kenton said. "It takes them other things I mentioned. Like the train and the stage."

They heard a rider plowing his way through the adjacent growth, then a man wearing a sheriff's badge broke clear.

Kenton looked momentarily startled. Then he simply stared and said, "We're rangers."

Castillo said, "You shouldn't be. Even for a ranger, this is outrageous."

Kenton studied his face, then said, "Sympathizing with your countrymen?"

Castillo said in a flat voice, "Not my countrymen, but of the same blood as me. That means something you maybe can't understand."

"Don't guess I can."

Castillo turned to Barnes. "Did you witness what he did here?"

This was a hard moment for Barnes. The sheriff was going to make trouble for Kenton. And Barnes could understand that. What he couldn't understand was his own reluctance to give an honest answer to the question.

Castillo was staring at him now, waiting.

So was Kenton. Then, as the silence held, Kenton's stare moved to the sheriff, and he said, "Did *you*?"

"You goddamn right I did. I saw it all!"

Barnes finally spoke. "I was watching from on top of the bluff. I couldn't hear what was said."

"What I'm asking," Castillo said, "is did you see him shoot down these men?"

Barnes said reluctantly, "I saw."

The sheriff turned to Kenton. "I'm taking you into Nogales on a murder charge."

Kenton laughed. "You'd never make it stick. I'm a lawman. And I'd plead self-defense in the line of duty."

Castillo only said, "You coming peaceful?"

"Why not?" Kenton said. "It's a shorter ride than the way we came." There was no worry showing on him.

But there was on Barnes.

With little talk between them, Castillo led the way to Nogales. Barnes and Kenton followed, each leading a bandit's horse with a stinking corpse thrown across its saddle.

Barnes was sickened by what had happened, Kenton appeared unconcerned, and Castillo brooded silently.

As they rode into the town, stretched north and south in a pass through some hills sparsely covered with desert grass, yucca, and some mescal, people stepped out of brick office buildings to stare at the dead bodies.

Sheriff Castillo looked neither right nor left. He headed directly for the Santa Cruz County Courthouse, a square, granite building with an aluminum gilded dome.

Barnes wondered fleetingly if the jail was as strong as this building looked.

There would likely be an arraignment. Whether Castillo could make his charge stick was a difficult question to answer.

Castillo seemed to be having some doubts himself. As soon as word had passed around town that the bodies brought in were those of the two desperados who had been raising so much hell lately in the Territory, most of the local citizens were praising the man who had put an end to them.

That put a halt on his intentions. Foremost in his decision was the bearing that his subsequent actions would have on his ability to be reelected.

Barnes had immediately wired Ryerson in Douglas, and the ranger captain's wire back to the sheriff that this was an internal matter had its effect. Ryerson had hinted strongly that he was capable of disciplining his men and that it would be wise for a first-term sheriff not to antagonize him, remembering that he was the commanding officer of a law-enforcement unit that had been created by the efforts of the governor.

Castillo, ever aware that no matter how capable he was in his job, he could not afford political enemies, dropped all thought of bringing charges. But it griped him that he did so. His Mexican blood was a big handicap in a country controlled by gringos.

Having to back down changed his anger toward Kenton to outright hatred.

They took the train from Nogales up toward Benson, then down to Douglas. They had wired Ryerson they were on their way, and he was at the depot, waiting for them.

His greeting was not effusive.

"Get your horses taken care of," he said, "then see me at headquarters."

Neither Barnes nor Kenton did more than nod. An exchange of words with the captain was not something Barnes looked forward to. Nor apparently did Kenton.

They got their mounts unloaded from a stock car and put up at the company's stables, then headed silently to Ryerson's office.

Just as they got there, Kenton said, "You think he's going to get tough about what happened?"

"What the hell do *you* think?" Barnes said.

They soon found out.

"Let me tell you what we're up against," Ryerson said as soon as they were seated. "Certain elements of our population—and the newspapers that cater to them—accuse us of being too harsh in our methods. Some local and county law officers, jealous that we're usurping their authority, oppose our presence here and resent that when we make an arrest they lose whatever reward money there might be.

"An even bigger threat to the continued existence of the rangers is the opposition party in the legislature that fought against our creation and who've never stopped trying to disband us. This segment continually cites the cost of maintaining us, as well as our tough policy.

"Needless to say what happened over there in the Santa Ritas handed them some big-bore ammunition."

Ryerson paused, and when he continued, his voice took on a near-strident edge: "Goddammit, Kenton, what you did over there was murder!"

"Murder, Cap? If it was, it was legal murder."

"Legal murder?"

"Same as in a war, Cap. Same as you done, going up San Juan Hill."

Ryerson gave him a long, baffled look. "War does strange

things to some men. I guess there are others like you." He paused. "Jake, I've got to let you go."

Kenton stared at him. "You saying it's for bad conduct, Cap?"

"I'm saying it's for the good of the service," Ryerson said.

For the first time, Kenton showed anger.

"It's your loss, Cap."

"That may be," Ryerson said. "I'm sorry, Jake."

Kenton got up, flicked a glance toward Barnes, and saw he wasn't going to defend him. His face hardened, and he seemed about to speak, but didn't.

He turned and walked out the door without saying another word.

After he was gone, Ryerson said, "I didn't mention that I heard some angry words again from Colonel Kosterlitzky."

"I supposed you would," Barnes said.

The captain was silent for a moment, then said, "The slaughtered men were Mexican nationals. There's another curious angle about the affair. I mean the two wanted men—their names were Bojorquez and Soto, remember?"

"Of course I remember, Cap."

"I asked that fool question for a reason. Kosterlitzky let slip there was another Rurale down there even more upset than he was. A Sergeant Soto. Same one you two had the earlier brush with."

"Same name as one of the men Kenton killed," Barnes said, frowning.

"Sergeant Soto's cousin."

Barnes shook his head. "Coincidences happen, don't they, Cap?"

"And that's a fact," Ryerson said.

Coincidences that could add up to trouble in the future, Barnes thought.

Like the one that had resulted in his having become teamed with Kenton.

CHAPTER 7

ALTHOUGH RANGERS ON assignments were frequently sent out in pairs unless the job seemed to call for a larger force, Ryerson did not give Barnes another partner right away.

Perhaps, Barnes thought, Ryerson wanted to see what he could do on his own, freed finally from his association with Kenton.

That suited Barnes. He owed his life to Kenton, but he felt only relief at being shed of him.

He was ready and eager to handle things his way.

He did not have long to wait. Within three days the captain had him back in his office.

Ryerson did not ask if he was ready for new action; he expected his men to be that way at all times. That's what they got paid a hundred dollars a month for. Ryerson expected them to earn it.

But Barnes was not quite ready for the chore Cap handed him.

"I've received phone communication from that rancher Covell recently. As you could expect, she remains disappointed that neither her cattle nor the money they were sold for by the rustlers were ever retrieved."

"You're going to send me down into Sonora again?"

Ryerson shook his head. "Too late for that. I told you the Mexican authorities are irate. Their attitude at this time would be total refusal to cooperate in any way, especially since this latest episode."

"Why are you mentioning the Covell ranch rustling, then?" Barnes said.

"I want you to go see the woman, try to placate her some-

67

what. She is hinting at sending a written complaint to our leading opponents in the legislature. Right now they've been complaining about the three thousand dollars a month it takes to keep us in existence."

Barnes said, "But it was a majority who voted for our formation."

"True," Ryerson said. "But fewer of those members that authorized us remain there. And new political opposition grows. That ranch woman's complaint could have a strongly adverse effect."

He was back in Elgin again.

Looking at the same storefront he'd last seen with Kenton.

Inside, the storekeeper recognized him at once. This time, though, his greeting was cool.

"You back?"

A fool question. Barnes did not answer it.

"Why, this time?" the man said.

"On the way to see Mrs. Covell," Barnes said.

"What about?"

"My business."

"You didn't do much for her last time you was here."

"Might be the reason I've come again."

The merchant took that in silence, then said, "I hope so. But I would have thought they'd have sent somebody else, was they going to."

"Well, they didn't," Barnes said. "How is she getting along?"

The merchant gave him a hard look. "Don't expect a warm welcome," he said.

Barnes held his stare for a long moment, then turned and walked out of the store.

The place looked the same. This time, as he rode up, an old, weathered cowhand emerged from the small bunkhouse and came walking toward Barnes. He was unarmed, but seemed to be hurrying his pace so as to intersect Barnes as he rode toward the ranchhouse porch.

Barnes turned toward him. As he drew close, he said, "Miz Covell about?"

The cowhand stopped a few feet from him, staring at his star.

"Arizona ranger," Barnes said

"I recall you from sight, last time you was here." The oldster's voice was flat. He hesitated, then gestured at the house.

When he said no more, Barnes reined around and started toward the house. He heard the old man walking just behind him.

He reached the porch and dismounted. The cowhand went up the steps, opened the door, and called inside, "Miz Jane, visitor!"

Barnes heard her voice inside, and a moment later she came to the doorway to peer out at him.

"You!" she said.

"Captain Ryerson sent me," he said.

"To try to explain what went wrong down in Sonora, I suppose."

"Something like that, I guess. But I believe he tried to tell you that."

"Yes, he tried."

"I was there," Barnes said. "Perhaps he thinks I can explain it better."

She thought over his words, then said, "All right. Come in."

As the old hand stood aside to let Barnes pass, she said to him, "It's all right, Tom."

"You want I should wait here?" Tom said.

"That won't be necessary," she said. She then led Barnes into the main room and gestured to a chair. She seated herself across from him.

"I was disappointed in the way I lost out on the rustled cattle," she said.

"Well, ma'am, I can understand that. I was disappointed, too. So was Captain Ryerson."

After a moment she said, "And your partner—was he disappointed?"

"Things just got out of hand when we met up with the rustlers."

"Out of hand," she said.

"It happens that way sometimes, ma'am."

"Sometimes," she said.

"Ma'am, each year we make hundreds of successful arrests. For a single company of only twenty-six men we believe we have reason to be proud. We are winning a battle against a vastly more numerous enemy of rustlers, holdup men, murderers, forgers, even opium dealers. And rapists, ma'am, a breed I hate worst of all."

"Where is your partner, Mr. Barnes?"

"He is no longer with the service, ma'am."

"He was responsible for what happened in Mexico, wasn't he."

"Things just got out of—"

"—hand." She paused. "Comrade loyalty is something I have heard discussed. My late husband had done a stint in the cavalry before we married. He made mention of it sometimes. Your ranger company seems to be patterned after the military."

"To a certain degree," Barnes said. "Our enlistment is twelve months, but most reenlist again and again. And our charter, I believe, reads that we're 'governed by the rules and regulations of the army of the United States, as far as the same shall be applicable.'"

She said, "What I was referring to is the seeming reluctance to place the blame on any specific member."

"Yes, there is that, too, I suppose," he said. "But our job

is a tough one, ma'am, and all of us make mistakes sometimes."

"You are trying to change my feelings," she said.

"I hope I can." He smiled. "That's why I was sent here."

"My dissatisfaction must have been very important to
your captain for him to detail a busy ranger to take time
and travel to explain."

"Ma'am, it's more than that. I've wanted to explain ever
since things went bad down there in Mexico."

"You cared that much?"

He said, "I did, ma'am. I kept thinking about the trust
you put in us to help you." He met her eyes when he spoke.
"Ma'am, pardon me for saying, but I kept thinking about
you too."

The look on his face brought a sudden color to her
cheeks.

He noticed, and feared he had gone too far.

"I meant no offense, ma'am."

She hesitated, then said, "I've taken none."

"I'm glad that's so."

The short silence that ensued was broken when she
turned away and said, "Will you have coffee?"

"I'd appreciate it."

There was a knock at the door, and she went to it.

Old Tom stood there, and said, "Everything all right,
Miz Jane?"

"Everything is fine, Tom."

"All right, Miz Jane."

She closed the door gently, turned, and went toward the
kitchen, avoiding Barnes's eyes.

He could hear her setting a pot of water on the wood-
stove and lighting the fire.

Presently she came back and resumed her seat, facing
him. "It'll take a bit for it to boil," she said.

"It takes a lot of nerve for a woman alone to run a
ranch," he said.

"There are other women who do it," she said.

"In this area?"

"No, not here."

"How long have you been doing so?"

"I lost my husband two years ago," she said.

"Big job for a woman alone," he said again.

"I have two hands that stayed on. In busy times I hire what help I can get."

"Tom is one of them?"

"Tom Weathers, and a man in his late forties, Matt Hayes. Both experienced cowhands. Matt's out working on fence today."

"Why do you keep on?"

"What else could I do?"

"Sell out. Get a town job somewhere."

"Doing what? Clerking in a store? I was doing that over in Sonoita when I met and married John Covell five years ago. This ranch he left me is the first thing I've ever possessed. My mother died years ago. My father was a miner and I kept house for him from early childhood. He was killed in a cave-in when I was eighteen, the year before I married." She paused. "When you've owned nothing all your life, a place like this, small as it is, is something to cherish."

He nodded. "I can see how that would be. My own dad was a sometime ranch foreman, various parts of the Territory, when I was growing up. He's gone now, also. Cowboying was mostly my trade too, till I got restless and hired on as a gun guard at a mine down near Cananea in Sonora. And then joined the rangers."

"Will you stay?" she said.

He was momentarily startled by the question.

She saw this, and smiled. "I didn't mean *here*," she said. "I meant in the rangers."

"Maybe. Until we are eventually disbanded. It was never

intended that we be a permanent force. Once we get the rampant outlawry under control, we'll be terminated."

"Do you think that's possible?"

"We're doing it, ma'am. It may take another three or four or five years. But we'll do it."

"But you must work at great risk. Four or five years is a long time."

"We will make Arizona Territory fit to become a state," he said. "That was the aim of Governor Murphy when he got the bill to create us through the legislative assembly in 1901."

"A worthy aim, I suppose," she said. She stood up. "The water is boiling. Excuse me." She moved toward the kitchen.

His eyes followed her trim figure. She was a fine-looking woman, he thought. John Covell had been a lucky man to have her.

A woman like her could be a reason to make a man decide on a settled life. Even an adventurous type drawn to a ranger's job. Most of the rangers were single men. Their roaming life on assignments was not compatible with a domestic relationship.

There were exceptions, but Cap Ryerson preferred his men footloose and fancy-free.

He was still thinking about this when she came back with a tray bearing cups of coffee.

She seemed to notice his preoccupation as she approached him. Some hint of intuition kept her silent as she placed his cup on a small table beside him.

He looked up and said, "Thank you."

"You were deep in thought," she said.

"Was I? Yes, I guess I was."

"Thoughts are private," she said. "I won't ask you what you were thinking."

"Just as well, ma'am," he said. And immediately saw the curiosity come into her face.

Wrong thing to say, he thought. He had a lot to learn about women.

She was silent, but he could see that her curiosity remained. He had a strange desire then to reveal to her what he had been feeling.

He said, "I was thinking how different the life of a settled man could be."

"When you and your comrades finally accomplish the job you've undertaken, you will think even more about it."

"That might be," he said. "It's odd, but until just now it was never on my mind."

He was merely stating a fact that occurred to him, but he saw her curiosity change now to a sort of pleased surprise.

She seemed about to make a comment, but stopped before she spoke.

He said, "We lead a life of constant action. We come to think there is no other way, I guess."

She nodded, but still did not speak.

Her silence seemed to drive him to continue talking.

"I'm boring you," he said.

She spoke quickly then. "No! Not at all. It is not often I have conversation with men. Except for Matt and old Tom." She paused, coloring slightly, and said, "I enjoy hearing the words of a younger man."

Then, as if ill at ease with what she'd said, she crossed over to seat herself apart from him.

"You have not gone into the details of what happened in Sonora," she said. "About my cattle."

Reluctantly, he said, "Briefly put, the rustlers were killed before we could learn who the cattle were sold to."

"And the money?"

"The rustlers had spent it, as far as we know. We found only a few pesos on them."

She frowned, but did not speak for a long moment.

Then she said, "Who killed them? You?"

He hesitated. Even now he hated to put specific blame on Kenton, even though he knew it was warranted.

"It was your partner," she said, "wasn't it?"

He nodded.

She said, "You say he is no longer a ranger?"

"That's right."

"And was his dismissal due to this?"

"It had considerable bearing on it."

"Considerable bearing," she said.

It was time to finish his assignment and leave, he thought. But he found it difficult to do so. He sat in silence, having finished drinking his second cup of coffee.

She had fallen silent, too.

It was the extended silence that finally made him put the question bluntly.

"Have I convinced you not to take your grievance to the politicians? They would use it against us in the assembly, and we think that would harm our effort to halt the wave of crime in the Territory."

She studied him for a long time.

She said finally, "All right. I agree."

"I appreciate that, ma'am."

When he left, a short time later, he felt certain he could trust her to abide by her agreement.

Where she was personally concerned, however, he was not sure of anything. Except that he had not wanted to leave.

CHAPTER 8

BARNES REPORTED IN by phone from Sonoita that he thought Jane Covell would not formally criticize the rangers for the handling of her case.

He hoped he had done better. He hoped he had convinced her that despite an occasional failure, twenty-six men wearing the star were doing a job above and beyond expectations.

Cap Ryerson listened carefully, then said, "Good enough."

Barnes said, "Shall I come in?"

"No. I've got an assignment for you up in the Gila Mountains. More cow stealing. Catch a train somewhere along the S.P. line and take it to Safford. You may have to go to Benson and wait for stock-car transportation for your horse. Your railroad pass is good for it. Phone or wire me when you reach Safford." Ryerson paused. "The spread getting rustled is owned by a rancher named Ruddock. There'll be folks in Safford can direct you to him."

"Right, Cap."

Barnes unloaded his horse at Safford, phoned Ryerson, and after verifying Cap's directions with a local justice of the peace, Sam Roberts, he headed north toward the foothill country beyond which rose the Gila range.

The country here was covered with greasewood, interspersed with tall, slim yuccas. As he neared the higher, rolling ground this gave way to decent grazing, and rounding a shallow curving valley he came upon the Ruddock ranch.

It was typically rustic, an average spread.

It was now early evening, and as he entered the ranch yard he heard the sound of the meal triangle. Four men left a bunkhouse and crossed toward the main dwelling. One of them turned his head, spotted Barnes, and spoke to the others.

Barnes was converging on them, but they did not stop until they reached the tie-rack near the house. He reached it only moments behind them. Barnes halted. He was wearing his badge in plain sight and was silent, waiting for any forthcoming comment.

Finally, one of them said, "Ranger, eh?"

Barnes nodded.

"You best light then, if you're hoping to find any grub left at the supper table." He did not smile as he spoke, nor did his companions.

"I'd be much obliged to do so," Barnes said. He swung down, tied his horse.

The spokesman gestured to a standing pump at the corner of the house. There was a tin cup on a chain and a soiled towel hung from a nail in the wood siding.

"Water there, ranger. Mess hall just beyond, round the side the building."

"Be with you in a couple of minutes," Barnes said.

He moved, trail stiff, toward the pump, and was passed by the others. Hungry men wait for no man, he thought, and gave himself a quick wash as he watched them enter a jutting addition to the house. He forsook drying with the towel, and a moment later entered himself.

The others were already seated; the yard spokesman said something to a heavyset older man who rose from his seat at the table's head as Barnes appeared.

He stepped toward Barnes, extending his hand. Barnes moved to him and shook it, saying, "Ranger Wes Barnes."

"Ed Rudock," the owner said. He gestured toward a couple of extra chairs against the wall. "Pull up one of those and get your share before these boys get it all."

"Be obliged," Barnes said.

The food was passed around the table, and there was a spell of no conversation as they all fell to eating.

The Chinese cook looked in once from his kitchen, then disappeared.

As they finished, the men started to get up.

"You boys stay a minute," Ruddock said, and they sat again. "This here is Ranger Barnes." He turned to Barnes, then nodded across the table. "Barnes, that fellow there that talked to you when you come up, is my foreman, Shad Yancey."

Barnes and Yancey exchanged stares, but neither spoke.

"These other boys, you'll learn their names working with them the next day or two."

Ruddock looked at Barnes. "That's what you got in mind, ain't it?"

Barnes said, "Yeah. Let me ride around your range like I'm a newly hired hand."

"He's here to try to find out where our calves are going," the rancher said.

Yancey spoke up. "He won't find out much riding around with that star on his shirtfront and wearing an arsenal."

"Badge goes in my pocket, as of now," Barnes said. "Colt goes in my saddlebag. Winchester stays in its scabbard, though. Just in case I see any coyotes killing calves."

"An undercover man," Yancey said. "Good luck."

"I may disappear for a couple of days now and then," Barnes said. "If I do, don't you boys worry about me."

"Ain't likely," Yancey said.

He rode the range close by for a couple of days, gradually working out into the backcountry a little. On the third day he asked Ruddock for a packhorse and provisions.

"Any other ranchers deeper in?" he said.

"No ranch headquarters," Ruddock said. "But it's free graze. At times strays are found from far-off places, but not often."

"Ryerson never mentioned your problem was mostly calf loss," Barnes said.

"Well, you know now," Ruddock said. Then he added, "You getting any ideas?"

"None except to keep looking."

"Have Yancey fix you up with a pack animal and what else you need," Ruddock said.

Two days later he was in a sharp-cut country of intersecting canyons and rugged slopes. It was mean terrain, he thought, and the graze here was not good. He'd left the best of that behind him.

It was country a man unfamiliar with could get lost in, and he climbed a high, steep shoulder for a vantage point from which to scout it.

It was then he saw a rider in the far distance below, driving a calf ahead of him. Even as he watched, the man and the calf disappeared into a ravine in the bottom of which Barnes thought he caught a glint as of sun on water.

He started his mount in that direction, though first belting on his gun.

He was a while getting there, not wanting to alert the rider by sound of rising dust.

Finally he approached the ravine into which the rider had gone. There was little more than a trickle of water escaping from somewhere above a few stagnating pools at its bottom.

Then he came to a sort of natural dam, formed years past by the caving-in of a ravine shoulder. It was lower on one side than the other and above this low section he glimpsed the top of some rough-timber fenceposts and barbed wire.

He turned his horse to climb the intersection of dam and

ravine side and dismounted before he reached the top. Leading the horse, he went on foot till he could cautiously peer over the crest.

A small grassy valley lay before him, with rim rock forming a natural wall around it. Here and there low spots in the rock had been filled in with more fencing. And at the far end of the valley a spring fed a small stream that gathered into a pool as it progressed. What overflow there was somehow seeped into the bottom of the ravine below.

The overflow wasn't much, because inside the valley were thirty or forty weaned calves drinking from the pond.

Barnes studied the scene for a long time, searching for the rider he had seen. At one point in a section of fence was a rough gate held shut by a a loop of heavy smooth wire. What appeared to be the calf he had seen driven was standing just inside it, as if recently shoved in and left.

He saw no sign of the rider.

Gone after another calf? he wondered. Or is he out there watching me?

He went to the gate and entered it and rode among the calves. Some had Ruddock's Circle R brand, others were unbranded. There was no sign of a branding fire in the area, and this told him that whoever had gathered these had a buyer somewhere for stolen cattle. There had been no apparent attempt to use a running iron to change the existing markings. Or to brand the brandless.

He returned to the gate and studied the ground beyond it.

There was a trail leading northward, that showed passage of small herds. It was obvious that the calves collected here in the little valley had been preceded by others.

So this was where the missing Ruddock calves were going. But up the trail to where?

He exited the gate, closing it securely behind him, and started following the sign of the earlier drives.

After a few miles the trail veered eastward.

He took a map of Arizona from a saddlebag and, guessing at his location, judged that the Gila Bonita River, a
creeklike tributary, lay in that direction. There had been
some gold mining in that area at one time, he believed.
Maybe there still was.

Two and a half hours' riding brought him in sight of
the stream.

The calf trail led to its side, with prints of cattle having
watered there. The trail then turned north, following the
creek. A few miles up he came to a cluster of weathered
wooden structures.

The trail ended at the beginning of the main street, and
there was a sign posted beside it: BROWN'S CAMP.

It was a small town, really. Up the street he could see a
saloon, barbershop, hotel, mercantile, and a butcher shop.
A sprawl of mine buildings clung on a steep barren shoulder, above and to the west.

It was the butcher's sign that caught his eye. He'd start
there.

He turned first and rode to where he could view the
back side of the row of businesses. Down past a clutter of
tin cans, discarded bottles and cartons, and various privies,
he spotted a small corral behind the butcher's shop. There
were four calves in the corral.

Waiting to be slaughtered, he thought, and made his way
through the scattered trash until he was close enough to
look for a brand on them, hoping to see a Circle R. Three
of them stood with their right rib cage exposed and were
free of markings.

The fourth faced the other way, and he pressed on until
he was far enough beyond the corral to see its far side.

There it was, Ruddock brand and all. That was going to
make his work easier, he thought, and turned toward an
open throughway to the street.

He had gone only a few paces when a man stepped out
of a rear door that faced the corral. He wore a holstered

gun belted around his waist, range garb, and a scowl on his black-bearded face. Barnes thought he could be the man he'd seen back in the Gilas.

The man with the gun called, "Hold on there! What the hell you doing back here?"

Barnes said, "These your calves?"

There was a short silence, then the man said, "You looking to buy?"

"Maybe. You looking to sell?"

"Maybe. I thought you was maybe looking to steal."

Barnes said slowly, "My guess is that's already been done."

"How so?"

"One's got a Ruddock brand."

"Ruddock sells cattle."

"Not calves, he don't."

"You a Ruddock hand?"

"Acting in that capacity."

"You got tall tones for a part-time hire."

Barnes let his gun hand hang, but reached with his rein hand up to his pocket and retrieved his ranger star. It was too far for the man to read it, but he could see the sun glint on it.

"A badge toter, then?"

"Ranger. You claiming ownership of this stock?"

"Ranger, eh?" the man said. He was still scowling, but now with worry. Finally he said, "Might be the butcher owns them."

"That the butcher shop behind you?"

"Yeah."

Barnes rode toward him. "Lift out your gun with your fingertips and drop it."

"What you going to do?"

"Do what I say," Barnes said.

The man did it, then repeated, "What you going to do?"

Barnes dismounted, looped his reins around a corral

rail, and walked forward. "We're going inside and have a talk with the butcher."

The man stood unmoving until Barnes was within an arm's reach. He then turned abruptly and led the way in.

They passed through a room with a couple of cutting tables. There was half a calf carcass hanging from a hook, ready for butchering.

They entered the shop beyond, and a chunky man with a ruddy face looked up from behind a display counter.

He appeared to be waiting. "Who you got there, Lute?"

"Fellow I told you I heard out there," Lute said.

"Bring him on in," the butcher said.

"He's doing the bringing," Lute said.

The butcher saw Lute's empty holster and said, "What the hell?"

"Reckon he'll do the talking," Lute said.

Barnes said, "Arizona Ranger. Looks like you got a market for veal in this town."

"I sell a little. Kind of breaks the monotony of eating beef. Some of the folks here like a change now and then."

"Where do you get your beef?"

"Comes in regular from the slaughterhouse at Morenci."

"You must get a real low price, to buy veal on the hoof and go to all the trouble of butchering it."

"What're you driving at?"

"One of those calves in your corral carries Ed Ruddock's brand."

"So? If he's a rancher, he could sell calves."

"He could," Barnes said. "But he doesn't."

"And how would you know that?"

"I just left him a few days ago. My packhorse out back has the same brand. A loan to me."

"So?"

"Who did you buy the calves from? I know it wasn't Ruddock."

The butcher exchanged glances with Lute. Then he said, "From him."

Lute said, "You son of a bitch!"

"What did you expect me to say?" the butcher said. "It's the truth."

"If it is," Barnes said, "then you're guilty of receiving stolen stock."

"That'd be damn hard to prove," the butcher said. "I deny it."

Barnes knew the man had a point there. Few cases like this ever resulted in a conviction. But he made no comment.

Instead, he said to Lute, "I'm taking you in to Safford."

"What for?"

"Rustling—what else?"

"You got a warrant?"

"This star I'm carrying is my warrant. There'll be another drawn up by Judge Sam Roberts when we reach Safford."

"I ain't sure that's legal."

"Take my word for it," Barnes said. "Lute your last name?"

"Yeah. Glen Lute."

"Where's your horse?"

"Out front. Say, what about my gun you made me drop. That's worth money."

"We'll get it. Empty of cartridges." Barnes turned to the butcher. "There'll be a Ruddock man or two along to recover those calves out back. Those dogies better still be there when they get here. Unless you're looking for trouble."

The butcher nodded. "I'll see it's so."

"I ain't ate all day," Glen Lute said.

Barnes was satisfied that he'd taken his man without violence. It was proof that Kenton's way was uselessly harsh, he thought.

"I'll stake you to a meal at the restaurant," he said to the rustler.

They started back, retracing the calf trail.

Lute said, "It'd be easier to follow the creek down. Twenty miles and we'd hit the road to Stafford."

"I want to report to the Ruddock ranch," Barnes said. "They can send out men to get the calves. Also to tell Ed Ruddock I've got you under arrest."

Lute's face had been showing concern, but now it deepened, showing sign of near panic.

Barnes noticed this and said, "I reckon you hate to confront the man you've been stealing from."

"It's more than that—" the rustler said, then clamped his mouth shut.

"What do you mean?"

"Never mind," Lute said.

Barnes shrugged.

They'd got a late start, and it was near sunset when they reached the little grassy valley where the calves were.

"We'll camp here," Barnes said.

"Good idea," Lute said. Aside from his understandable concern, he'd been a peaceful-enough prisoner. Barnes had felt no need to put manacles on him.

During the hours of close riding contact, Barnes had realized the man was in his late twenties. Lute's dark, heavy beard made him look older.

He was glad the man had put up no resistance.

And he was glad he was free of Jake Kenton as a partner.

Barnes had emptied Lute's handgun and rifle of cartridges back at the mining camp. He'd also made a search of his saddlebags and retrieved a spare box of shells from each. A body search had revealed no more.

That night, he slept with his own and Lute's weapons beside him. Lute, now manacled and ankle-tied, was bedded down in a blanket roll a few yards away.

* * *

Glen Lute lay quiet, listening to the regular breathing of his captor. He had done this for an hour before he began to shift slightly, moving his manacled hands out to grasp one of his discarded boots that lay beside him.

Lucky for him, the goddamn ranger had allowed him to remove the footwear before he'd tied his feet.

It was the right boot he reached for: that was the one with the slim-sheathed knife sewn tightly inside its shank. A hideout knife, an idea that he'd gleaned from a Mexican fellow inmate at Yuma Territorial prison while Lute was doing three years for cattle theft. He'd finished his time six months back, and he had no intention of ever doing time again. Once was too much. Even if he had to kill to prevent it, something he had never done before.

He managed to draw the blade from the tight sheath. The ranger was too easy; you'd have thought he'd think to examine the boots. Too bad for him, Lute thought. Too bad for me too. What he was about to do he regretted, even before it was done. It was the thought of Yuma that drove him on. He began to work the blade against the ankle thongs.

The thongs gave way and he reached for his boots. He had trouble drawing them on with his manacled hands. So much so, that he lay still again, listening for any sign of the ranger's awakening.

Still grasping the knife in both hands, he began to move cautiously toward the sleeping figure.

Barnes suddenly stirred restlessly, as if bothered by something in his dreams.

Lute halted in a crouched stance above him, the slim-bladed knife poised in his hands above Barnes's blanket-covered chest.

At that moment Barnes's eyes opened and must have caught the moon-glint on the steel because Lute sensed his reaching for the revolver at the blanket's edge.

And still he hesitated, knowing he had only a second to act.

The gun came free of the blanket, just as Lute let the knife drop harmlessly from his grip and cried out, "No!"

The blast of the gun drowned out his cry. Its bullet caught him navel high.

Half-crouched as he had been, he pitched face forward across Barnes's body.

Barnes threw him off with a frantic heave and leaped to his feet, gun still in his grip.

There was just enough moonlight that he could see Lute's face, see the faint movement of his lips.

And hear the last audible words he spoke.

"I couldn't do it," Lute said.

These words began to bother him as he headed toward the Ruddock place with the body.

Did Lute mean Barnes was too fast for him?

Or did he mean that, at the last moment, he'd had a change of heart about killing Barnes?

If it was the latter, then young Lute had died needlessly.

Just as a lot of Kenton's victims had.

CHAPTER 9

HE RODE INTO the Ruddock ranch yard with Lute's body draped over his mount's saddle.

It was the foreman, Shad Yancey, who saw him first. Yancey eyed the mount sharply.

Then, as Barnes closed in to tie up, Yancey stepped near and lifted the head of the dead man enough to stare at the features.

"Jesus!" he said. "You killed young Lute."

"You knew him?"

"He worked here a while back. We had a hand laid up a few weeks. Lute drifted by and the old man hired him to fill in temporary." He paused. "He was a damned good kid, and I hated to see him go when the need was over."

"Kid?" Barnes said.

"Twenty-two," Yancey said. "I reckon he raised that beard to look older." Again he paused. "Goddammit! Did you have to kill him?"

Barnes did not answer at once.

It was a question he had been asking himself ever since it happened.

Was he as trigger happy as Jake Kenton, when the chips were down? If he had waited a second later when he saw Lute with the knife . . .

It was too late now to do it over.

Yancey's eyes were hard. He was waiting for his answer.

"I had to kill him," Barnes said. "Why else?"

"I'd like to hear the details of it," Yancey said.

"Come along, then. Ruddock will want the story, too."

"That he will," Yancey said. "He felt like me about the kid."

First, though, they untied Lute's body and took it to a shed. None of the other hands were around to see this.

Yancey then led the way back to the house in silence and entered Ruddock's office. Ruddock looked up from an open ledger on his desk.

"That ranger is back," Yancey said.

"Show him in."

Barnes heard his words and stepped through the door.

Yancey said, "He brought in a dead man."

"Who?" Ruddock said. "A rustler?"

"Glen Lute," Yancey said bitterly.

"Lute! Some damn rustler killed Lute?"

"No," Yancey said. "A damn ranger did."

Ruddock's face showed shock. Then he said to Barnes, "You?"

"I had to do it," Barnes said, meeting the rancher's eyes.

Ruddock kept staring. Finally he said, "Tell me about it."

Barnes told him, trying not to feel defensive as he did.

They buried Lute a distance from the ranch house. None of those engaged in the digging—not Ruddock, Yancey, or Barnes—showed any expression as it was done.

The mixed feelings were too great for that.

Afterward they saddled up and rode back to the little valley where the calves were penned, Barnes leading the way.

Ruddock brought along a couple of extra hands to help Yancey drive the calves back to home graze. Ruddock himself had belted on a gun.

"I'm going on to that mining camp," he said to Barnes. "That's where me and that crooked butcher will have it out."

"I'd best show you how to get there," Barnes said, and fell in beside him.

They rode mostly in silence.

Once, Ruddock said, "A good kid, taken the wrong turn."

It didn't make Barnes feel any better.

The four calves were still in the butcher's corral. Barnes's threat had apparently had its effect.

He followed as Ruddock eyed the stock, then dismounted, tied his horse to the corral, and barged into the rear doorway of the shop.

Barnes noted the hanging half-carcass of a calf was now gone from the cutting room, but he said nothing. It would have spoiled by now anyway.

The butcher looked up, startled, as they reached the shop proper.

Before he could speak, the rancher said, "I'm Ruddock."

He had his hand on the butt of his gun as he said it.

The butcher's florid face turned pale.

"I'm agreeable to a settlement," he said.

"You damn well better be," Ruddock said.

"Yes, sir, Mr. Ruddock."

"A hundred dollars a head for those in your corral," Ruddock said.

"That's kind of steep!"

"How many others did you butcher?"

"There wasn't any others, Mr. Ruddock."

Barnes said, "There was part of one hanging in the back room, last time I was here."

"Oh, yeah," the butcher said. "I was forgetting that one."

"And probably a lot of others," Ruddock said. "Better make it two hundred dollars each for the five we know about."

"That ain't right!"

Barnes said, "I can get a warrant for your arrest, if you'd rather."

"No, I'll pay," the butcher said, and moved toward a safe in the corner.

Later, as Barnes and the rancher mounted up to ride their separate ways, Ruddock to his ranch, Barnes to take the direct road to Safford, Ruddock said, "Wasn't for crooks like him, there wouldn't be no rustling."

Barnes tended to agree.

"Nor good kids gone wrong," Ruddock said bitterly.

Back in Douglas, Captain Ryerson took Barnes's report and said, "You handled the assignment well."

Barnes had different feelings, but did not give voice to them.

"Damn-fool rustler was a killer for sure," Ryerson said, "to come at you with a knife when you were sleeping."

Barnes remained silent.

"It looks like you work well alone, Wes. So I'm going to keep you that way for the time being. Not all my men have that ability. Some do better with a partner, but when I've only got twenty-six men to handle all the pressing assignments, that can be a problem."

"You ever hear anything about Jake?" Barnes said.

"Kenton? No, he seems to have dropped from sight."

"Well, what's my next job?"

Ryerson shuffled through several papers, withdrew one, and scanned it thoughtfully.

While he did, he said, "This concerns more border trouble."

"Rustling again?"

"Not this time. I've got eight rangers working regularly now with the Arizona Cattle Growers Association. This is a different kind of problem." He paused. "I recall your last experience in Mexico, and that ought to give you strong motivation on this one."

Barnes waited.

Ryerson said, "Yaqui Indians."

"Yaquis?"

"Damned near killed you, didn't they?"

"They thought they had a reason," Barnes said.

"They always think they have a reason when they start acting up," Ryerson said. "But this latest rebellion of theirs against the Mexican government is small but bloody."

"What business is it of ours?"

"We once again have patched up our cooperative relations with the Mexican officials in Sonora. In return, they ask—demand, in fact—that we put a stop to the clandestine sales of arms and ammunition to the Yaquis that is fueling their bloody rampages."

"Sales by who?" Barnes said.

"The Mex officials claim they have information that American merchants in Nogales, Bisbee, and other border towns are profiteering by supplying them."

"Is that true?"

Ryerson shrugged. "That's for us to find out."

"Meaning me?"

"Meaning you."

"Where would I start?"

"Try Bisbee," Ryerson said.

Barnes rode the twenty-five miles to Bisbee. It was one of the liveliest of mining towns, eight miles north of the border. A huge lode of ore was owned by the Copper Queen Mining Company. And there were others.

Miners and mining men had been attracted from all over the world. Eastern mining engineers had brought their wives out and built fine homes here.

But there was another side to the town: riotous dance halls, whorehouses, and saloons lined Brewery Gulch, which intersected the main street of the business section.

Merchants thrived. But some, it appeared, were greedy enough to seek additional, illegal, ways to increase their profits.

This was what Barnes had been sent to investigate. And he was aware that Bisbee's riotous underworld detested the rangers. And had from the time of their formation.

It was nearing evening when he arrived; he put his mount up at a livery and took a room at the Copper Queen Hotel.

After a supper he made a walking tour of some of the shops. He had pocketed his badge when he'd left Douglas. This was undercover work, and one reason Ryerson had chosen him for the assignment had been his being a stranger to the town. He spent considerable time getting familiar with the location of types of merchants he thought might be inclined toward arms smuggling. There were hardware stores that stocked guns and three gun shops that repaired as well as sold them. He'd start checking them out in the morning.

When he did, he immediately ran into a setback.

The clerk in the first place he entered, one of the gun shops, recognized him, calling him by name. He was a young man.

"Morning, Ranger Barnes."

Barnes studied him, but could not recall ever seeing him.

The clerk said, "I was working in Morenci when you and your partner shot the bank bandits."

Barnes cursed silently. So much for working undercover, he thought.

He said, "That right?"

"You still got the same man siding you?"

Barnes shook his head.

"Yeah," the clerk said. "I recall hearing somewhere that they booted him out of the ranger outfit. Is that so?"

"He left," Barnes said.

"I didn't mean to pry," the clerk said. "What can I do for you, sir?"

"Just looking around."

"Want to buy a gun?"

"I've got a gun."

"Sure. Well, you're welcome to look," the clerk said. "My name is Frederick. Bill Frederick. I got a lot of respect for you rangers."

"Kind of an uncommon feeling in this town, way I hear it," Barnes said.

"Amongst some people maybe," Frederick said. "Not all."

"Glad to hear that," Barnes said. "I may drop in again sometime." He was surveying some display cases. "Looks like you've got a fine selection of arms here."

"We think so," Frederick said. "Pleasure to see you, sir."

Barnes nodded and left. Friendly fellow, he thought. Maybe too friendly.

As he stepped away from the storefront he glanced back to read again the name of the place: Gulch Gun Shop. Odd name, he thought.

His next stop was Graff's Hardware, which he recalled from the previous evening had an outside sign boasting a list of nearly all the popular makes of handguns and rifles.

The man who greeted him was gaunt and middle-aged, with graying hair and a preoccupied expression. He stood behind a counter as he nodded once to Barnes.

Barnes said, "Your sign out there indicates you carry quite an inventory of firearms."

"I've probably got whatever you need."

Barnes's eyes swept the long narrow store. It was filled with the usual assortment of hardware items, but one wall gave about ten yards of space to tall, shallow, glass-fronted cases in which weapons were racked in rows.

"Sell many?"

"Why do you ask?"

"Just curious."

"Mostly as a convenience for my customers. I'm primarily in the hardware business."

"Yes, of course," Barnes said. "You must be Graff."

"My name. Were you interested in weapons or hardware?"

"To be frank," Barnes said, "neither, today. Your gun ad out front aroused my curiosity, and I thought I'd take a look."

He walked over and studied the weapon display closely. It told him nothing specifically. There was a sizable selection of makes and models, as advertised.

He could feel the proprietor watching him as he mentally catalogued some of the inventory.

He turned to find Graff scowling.

Was he suspicious of Barnes's presence? Did he too know Barnes's identity?

Or was he simply irritated that Barnes was wasting his time, looking with no intention of buying, like a lot of other gun buffs who came into his store?

Graff's intent stare decided him to leave.

"May see you again, if I need a weapon," he told the shop owner, and headed for the door.

As he exited, he heard no sound of Graff answering.

There was another gun shop, just off Main Street, which Barnes had bypassed earlier because it was not yet opened for the day.

It was situated near the corner of OK Street, which paralleled Brewery Gulch and was a short distance across Main from the Southern Pacific Railroad station.

Predictably, the sign above it read THE OK GUN SHOP.

It now appeared open for business, and Barnes made his way toward it.

Inside was a man of perhaps thirty, whom Barnes pegged at first as a Mexican. The man spoke English without an accent, and was neatly groomed and dressed.

"Good morning, sir," he greeted Barnes. "Our first customer of the day. I hope."

"Just looking around," Barnes said.

"You are welcome to do that."

Barnes was drawn to the smiling face, and a closer look surprised him as he saw now the Indian cast to the man's features.

The man took note of his scrutiny and said, "Why do you stare, my friend?"

"I meant no offense," Barnes said.

"You see my Indian blood?"

"You appear well educated," Barnes said. He felt slightly embarrassed by the question.

"I had some schooling in Tucson. I was born near there."

A thought came to Barnes. There were Yaquis who had over the years found asylum in Arizona, fleeing Mexico. But he said, "You are Papago?"

"Papago? No. Although some of my people once found refuge on the Papago reservation. I was born in Pascua, a little settlement of Yaquis, east of Tucson. In Tucson I received some schooling."

"Yaqui, then?"

"And proud of it."

"You have a right to be," Barnes said.

"Thank you, sir. Not all agree with you."

Barnes sought now to change the conversation, and said, "I have some interest in guns, and came in to browse around to see what you have here."

"Please feel free to do so," the Yaqui said. "I also repair guns, if you need such service."

"I'll keep that in mind," Barnes said.

After a bit he tired of his pretext, and driven by investigative urge, he gambled on a more direct interrogation.

"You say your people were refugees from Mexico. But you are American born and raised. The fact makes me a little curious about your feelings."

"Feelings?"

"About the current Yaqui unrest in Sonora."

The man eyed him sharply, then said, "Might I ask what are your own feelings?"

Barnes said, "I have long had an amount of sympathy for your people."

The Yaqui's sharp glance had not lessened. "My people? But I am American."

"But your people weren't."

"I will tell you this," the gun repairman said. "I have no direct interest in what goes on below the border. Sympathy, of course, as you say you have."

"I understand," Barnes said. "You have satisfied my curiosity."

And so it went throughout that day, as Barnes visited other businesses that might be suspect. The investigation had given him things to think about, nothing more.

He headed back toward the hotel a short way up on the west side of Brewery Gulch.

There was a saloon just below it, and as he was passing, he was startled to see a familiar figure exiting the swinging doors.

Barnes halted and stared back as Jake Kenton stopped on the porch and looked down at him.

"Been a while, Wes."

"Yeah, it has." Barnes studied Kenton's face for sign of resentment. He saw none, and was relieved. "How's it going, Jake?"

"Good enough. And with you?"

"Passable."

"I was just leaving," Kenton said. "But come on in and have a drink for old-times' sake."

"Sure," Barnes said, and stepped up on the porch to join him.

They shook hands, then entered the place and moved without speaking to find a spot at the crowded bar. Once there, Kenton held up two fingers for the barkeep, who placed a bottle and a couple of glasses before them, then poured drinks.

"Wes, it's damn good to see you," Kenton said.

"Glad that's so," Barnes said. "You must have left Douglas right away after that last session in Cap's office. I looked for you, but you were gone."

"Didn't want to hang around where I wasn't wanted," Kenton said. "Always been my way."

"So what're you doing now?"

Kenton lowered his voice. "I got a good thing going, Wes. But I can use some help. And you could fit in right well."

"Hell, I'm still wearing the star."

"Don't see it on you."

"Undercover," Barnes said.

"That fits, too. Keep it that way," Kenton said.

"How so?"

They were hemmed in on either side by other patrons, and Kenton said, "I can't tell you here. Is there someplace we can talk?"

"I'm staying at the hotel up the street."

"Drink up then, and we'll go there."

Barnes wasn't sure he wanted that. He hesitated before saying with suppressed reluctance, "All right."

At the hotel he led the way to his room.

Almost at once, Kenton said, "You remember the trouble we had in Sonora with those damn Yaquis?"

"How can I forget?"

"And you must have heard they're raising still more hell down there now."

"I heard something about it," Barnes said.

"Don't fool with me, Wes. I know why you're here. I guessed when I saw you making the rounds of gun dealers today. I stayed back far enough to hope you wouldn't spot me. That kid in the Gulch Gun Shop remembered me from Morenci. He was suspicious, too."

"That couldn't have been enough to make you guess," Barnes said.

"No. I had an inside tip from another ranger Ryerson let go for drunkenness. He heard the rumor from an old compadre with a loose tongue."

"Cap should fire that one too," Barnes said with some heat.

"I agree," Kenton said. "But what you're doing could fit in with what I'm doing."

"And what's that?"

"I've been riding the line out of Naco lately. Hell, that's where the transactions take place. I knew it from hanging around this town for a time."

"Then you know who the suppliers are?"

Kenton did not answer the question. Instead, he said, "Look, I've struck a deal with the Sonoran government for forty percent on all the contraband that I can confiscate. I was working with an American customs officer. He got laid up with a bullet wound during our first raid on gunrunners as they crossed the border, east of Naco.

"They had a wagonload of weapons and ammunition, with a driver and four riders guarding it."

"Sounds like big odds," Barnes said.

"Not for you and me, Wes," Kenton said. "And there's money to be made."

"I'm not interested in money."

"You're interested in stopping gun sales, ain't you?"

"Yes. And I can do that if you tell me who the local suppliers are. And that's a hell of a lot less risky."

"May be," Kenton said, his face hardening. "But money is the thing with me now." His voice was suddenly bitter. "I was on the side of the law and gave it everything I had. And they booted me out of the force. That changed my thinking. From now on I'm getting all I can for my talents."

"With a gun," Barnes said.

"What else?"

"I'm sorry to hear that, Jake," Barnes said.

"Well, that's the way it is," Kenton said. "It's my way or none."

Barnes debated with himself. If he took Kenton up on his offer, he could learn something about the smuggling operation.

On the other hand his conscience stood in the way of his feigning acceptance of the offer with no intention of following through.

He had to hand it to Kenton for guts. The man was fearless when it came to gunplay: he seemed to thrive on it. And what he was doing was likely to give him plenty of opportunity to engage in it.

Barnes had his own share of courage, he believed. But he was not without fear when the bullets flew. He sure as hell wasn't like Kenton.

He decided to play a waiting game. He'd keep watching the local gun dealers. And he'd observe Kenton, see what moves he made. He'd try to keep conversing with him. Sooner or later he might give something away.

A few days went by, with Kenton managing to avoid him.

Occasionally he caught sight of Kenton hanging around the Southern Pacific depot at times when a train was due.

Was he expecting someone? Barnes wondered. A new partner for his border raiding? Or, the thought hit him suddenly, a shipment of some kind?

The thought came as he watched a freight car being unloaded. It was a day when Kenton had not appeared. He strolled over to examine the cargo stacked on the depot loading platform. There were boxes of all kinds and shapes. He got near enough to see the addresses inked on some of them. All to various businesses in Bisbee.

His eyes fastened on what appeared to be a wagonload of wooden boxes bearing a shipper's address in Tucson. They were also inked with the notice HANDLE WITH CARE: SEWING MACHINE PARTS. They were addressed to Dragoon Appliance Co., Bisbee, with an added stamp: HOLD FOR COMPANY PICKUP.

In the days he had walked the streets of the town Barnes did not recall encountering any business by that name.

He hunted up the S.P. agent behind a counter in the depot.

The man looked up inquiringly. "Yes?"

"I'm a little curious. I see there's a shipment on the dock for the Dragoon Appliance Company. I didn't know there was a company with that name in this town."

"Well, no, there isn't," the agent said. "You might have noticed the boxes say to hold here for pickup. They send their own wagon in from some little town I didn't know existed, southeast of here someplace. Called Double Wells, one of their drivers told me once."

"Must sell a lot of sewing machines," Barnes said.

"That what they got this time? Well, sometimes it's other things. Their wagon is usually in within a couple days. I guess they're sent a letter from Tucson when to expect a shipment here."

The station man paused, eyeing the range garb worn by Barnes. "You looking to buy a sewing machine?"

"No," Barnes said. "Hardly. But thanks for satisfying an old cowpoke's idle curiosity."

"Yeah," the agent said, his interest changing as he went back to checking through a sheaf of bills of lading.

Barnes left quickly.

Sewing machine parts, Barnes kept thinking. Why did that description on the boxes arouse his suspicions so strongly?

It took a while, but it came to him. In a novel he'd read,

by the war correspondent and fiction author Richard Harding Davis, this same labeling had been used by Central-American revolutionists—to disguise shipments of arms.

Could this be the case here?

The way to find out, he thought, was to keep watching for a wagon to come pick up the shipment.

CHAPTER 10

HE TOOK UP his vigil from the Post Office Plaza, a small flat a few hundred yards west of the railroad station.

There was a livery stable just east of the depot, and he briefly considered transferring his mount from where it was stabled near the hotel. He had discovered Jake kept his horse here.

He was still thinking about this when he saw a wagon appear from beyond the station and pull up next to the loading dock. It was too late then to change, and he sauntered toward the four-horse-drawn vehicle.

A driver and a swamper got down, went into the depot, and returned with the station agent, who had papers in his hand.

Barnes was near enough to observe and halted his approach by a nearby storefront. After a brief discussion, the agent went back inside, and the two men began carrying the wooden cases to the wagon's bed.

As soon as they were loaded, they got the team underway and drove off in the direction they had come.

Barnes turned up Brewery Gulch toward where his horse was stabled.

He got it saddled, paid what was owed for its keep, got his gear from the hotel, and rode off at a fast trot.

The road led southeasterly through the hills, then turned south.

When almost at once, Barnes came within sight of the wagon kicking up dust in the distance, he wasn't surprised.

The surprise came when he saw the wagon was followed by a rider, several hundred yards behind. Barnes had come up close enough to discern something familiar about the horseman. When he did, he quickly halted his mount and waited for the other rider to gain more lead.

He couldn't be sure, but he was halfway certain that the man following the wagon was Jake.

He stayed back now and guided his horse by the wagon's dust. They were taking the road to the border town of Naco.

Then, abruptly, the dust was gone.

He moved ahead even more cautiously, wary that the others might have halted. But eventually he saw that was not so.

They had simply turned into another pass that branched off to the east. Then it too turned south.

It came to Barnes now that they could be headed from some desolate border crossing a few miles ahead, but far enough east to be free of Naco customs agents, Mexican or American.

He continued trailing them, thinking back to the operation across the boundary line that Kenton had outlined to him, with the Sonoran officials paying forty percent on all confiscated arms.

Was Jake going to attempt to hijack the wagonload alone?

The road they now followed was no more than two wagon-wheel ruts; Barnes couldn't tell if it had had prior use, or if the driver was breaking new ground as he crossed a long stretch of flat desert, barren of all but mesquite and catclaw clumps.

Farther off to the southeast, Barnes could see what appeared to be a mound of rocks that could be a boundary marker.

He threw a routine glance toward the west, not expecting to see another marker because they were many miles apart. What he did see was dust rising as if stirred up by a rider or riders. Or it might be simply a desert whirlwind.

He quickly discounted the latter, as the dust cloud halted at the spot where he assumed the wagon to now be.

The wagon and the riders then moved on together into Mexico.

Escort riders was the thought that struck him then. Gun guards for the shipment.

Then, as he saw Kenton cross the line, another rider came from the west to join *him*. Had the American customs officer, who'd been wounded, recovered so quickly? The one whom Kenton had tried to recruit Barnes to replace?

He was beset by another question: If he was able to see all this ahead of him, why hadn't Kenton noticed him trailing behind? It would be only routine for Kenton to cast an occasional glance at his backtrail.

The answer could be that Kenton was aware he was being followed, but for reasons of his own did not care.

As Barnes rode up to the boundary, those ahead were temporarily obscured from his vision as they rounded a cluster of low-lying knolls sparsely dotted with greasewood and sage. This might be a spot where transfers were made, as Kenton had mentioned earlier.

As he was pondering this, gunshots sounded.

He kicked his horse into a gallop. As he came into sight of the halted wagon, he saw the battle taking place.

Next to the wagon, and partly shielded by the shipping boxes piled on the bed, were the driver, his helper, and two dismounted guards.

All were armed and firing at two attackers hidden behind a low-lying hummock of sand and scattered rocks.

From where he had halted north of the hummock, Barnes had an open view of this pair. One was unmistakably Kenton, and the other was a man wearing a badge. Both were answering the fire with revolver shots of their own.

So this was the action that Kenton had described to him and tried to draft him for. There was money to be had here, Kenton had said. There was also death to be had, Barnes was thinking. But the possibility of death was never something to deter Kenton.

Right now, shooting to kill the men at the wagon, Kenton would be experiencing nothing but gratification. But there were four-to-two odds the gratification would not last.

To Barnes, this grew to a certainty, as he saw the way the gun guards handled their weapons. Professionals.

Staring again at Kenton and his companion with the badge, he saw that the latter carried his left arm in a sling.

God! he thought. The customs officer was as wild as Kenton was. Taking part in an attack on a superior armed escort when he had only one good wing!

The thought made urgent a decision on Barnes's part of what to do.

True, the man with the customs badge was a lawman of sorts, no matter what his personal motive. And those with the wagon were illegally smuggling in guns to foment rebellion against a duly constituted government, recognized by the United States.

And to stop such smuggling was the assignment given Barnes by Ryerson.

But above all, it was the memory of Kenton's saving him from the Yaquis that sent him into action.

He turned east and spurred his mount into a run, not wasting time to circle wider, bent on reaching a point where he could attack Kenton's foes from behind. Knowing it made him an instant, though running, target.

Immediately shots were directed his way. He was at long range for the handguns and made it partway before one of them ran to his horse, jerked a carbine from his saddle boot, and sent a burst of shots that kicked up sand directly in front of Barnes, as he probed to find the distance to lead.

Barnes got far enough east to reach a shallow ravine,

into which he plunged, turning south so as to come abreast of the wagon.

In the saddle, his head and shoulders were still exposed to the guards.

He dismounted, dropping the reins, and crawled up the bank to peer over the top.

Both of the escort gunmen now had carbines in their hands, although the driver and the swamper had only handguns.

Damn fools, these two, Barnes thought. Apparently they had relied on the guards for protection. Would they try to open a shipment box? he wondered. Not likely, with bullets flying about them and probably no tools handy.

He slid his own rifle over the rim and began firing to further discourage any such attempt. He heard a fusillade from the side beyond his target as Kenton and his partner opened up with rifles.

With Barnes participating, the odds were now three rifles against two, with the driver's and the swamper's short-range weapons effective only against Kenton's side.

But they kept blasting away at the hummock, trying at least to disturb their assailant's aim.

The two escort riders, now lying prone, were concentrating on a duel with Barnes.

That made it two to one against him, he thought ruefully, changing his estimate of his chances.

He was a damn fool for getting into the fray, he told himself.

But somehow, if he had the choice again, he knew he'd do the same. Such was the weight of the obligation he felt he owed Kenton.

It made him curse, even as he fired a shot that caught one guard in the right shoulder, so that he dropped his carbine and went face flat into the dirt, writhing in pain.

One out of it, Barnes thought. He may ride out of this, but he won't be firing that weapon here again.

From the other side came a shot from the hummock that hit the swamper as he raised to fire over the wagon bed. It must have hit him high in the chest or in the head, because it drove him backward to sprawl face up and unmoving.

That's when the driver, in a desperate token of surrender, pulled a handkerchief from a pocket and waved it high enough to be seen.

Surprisingly, there was no shot from the hummock to try for his hand. Maybe Kenton is thinking of a need for the driver, Barnes thought.

He fired at the remaining guard and missed.

As the guard aimed toward him for a return shot, the other, wounded guard reached out to him, tugging at his clothing, as if in remonstration.

Barnes saw this and held his fire.

He watched as the two appeared to consult for a moment. Then the one with the rifle raised it with the barrel pointed skyward and brandished it back and forth.

Barnes called out, "You surrendering?"

"My buddy, he's hurt bad. You let us quit?"

"Heave that weapon away from you," Barnes yelled. "But stay down. Tell the driver to do the same!"

"Yeah, we do it!" the guard yelled back.

Barnes went to his horse, mounted, and picked a way up the ravine bank, keeping his eyes on those at the wagon. Not till he drew close did he relax at all, when he could see for certain they had complied with his order.

He said, "All of you stay low while I talk with the others."

The unwounded guard was not young, not old. He looked tough, though, not like the kind to give up.

He said to Barnes, "Them behind the hummock are on the same side as you, ain't they?"

"I hope so," Barnes said.

"What the hell," the guard said. "I wouldn't have quit, wasn't for Frank here bleeding bad, and asking me to."

Barnes looked down at the wounded man. There was

blood welling out of his shoulder. "Try to stop the flow," Barnes said.

The driver handed the guard the handkerchief he had earlier waved, and the guard pressed it against the wound.

Barnes was in plain sight of the two still behind the hummock. He saw Kenton raised up over the edge, watching him.

Kenton yelled, "What's going on, Wes?"

"It's over," Barnes said.

"Who says?"

"I say."

"Well, we need the driver, all right. But I'd just as soon put a bullet in that gunslinger."

"I already promised him no."

"By what right did you do that?"

"By the right of this ranger star I'm carrying."

"Ranger?" the guard said.

"All right!" Kenton called.

Presently he and the customs agent appeared, mounted. They rode over, each holding a revolver in hand.

The guard said harshly, "Tell them to put up them damn guns!"

As Kenton drew close, he said, "I only need the driver."

Barnes knew his meaning. He said, "You get the driver. But we're going to get the wounded one on his horse, and the other's going to lead him into Naco to a doctor."

Kenton stared at him hard for a long time, and Barnes stared back.

Finally, Kenton said, "Wes, you're too soft for the job you've got."

"Matter of opinion," Barnes said.

Kenton shrugged. "For old time's sake, have it your way. The wagon is what we want. And the driver. We got us a load of contraband to collect our percentage from the Sonora politicos."

"So be it."

"You could be getting a cut," Kenton said.

"Mine will be when I cut off the suppliers we trace out of Tucson," Barnes said.

Kenton showed no expression. But he shrugged and said, "Well, me and my partner got this load we can collect on." He paused. "You wouldn't try to take it away from us, would you, Wes?"

Barnes did not answer at once. But finally he said, "No. Not this time. But it may be your last."

"Don't count on it," Kenton said.

Barnes nodded, and said, "Yeah."

CHAPTER 11

BARNES SAT IN his saddle, watching the wagon with the driver—escorted by Kenton and his partner—disappear southward.

He felt he was making a mistake, letting them consummate their profitable deal with the Sonorans.

But it would have been a worse mistake to have tried to stop them. To try to do that would have meant the death of Kenton or of himself. Because that's the way Kenton was.

He had learned basically that the arms dealers were centered in Tucson and the route of at least one of their pipelines, though a losing one for them due to the action of Kenton.

Actually, Kenton, for selfish reasons, was providing a service more effective than the rangers had yet been able to do.

He'd report what he'd learned to headquarters. It would be Cap Ryerson's job to give the orders from there.

As the wagon and the riders vanished from his sight, he had a disturbing feeling that Kenton was headed for trouble.

It wasn't like the Sonoran officials to continue to pay for contraband arms. Why not just confiscate them for themselves?

Barnes felt a wry emotion as he considered what Kenton's reaction would be to that.

It could be violent, he thought.

The American customs officer, Joe Kaler, said to Kenton, "That ranger acquaintance of yours, he could make trouble for us."

"Maybe," Kenton said. "But he helped us out of a scrape back there."

"He did that. Known him long?"

"Long enough."

"Ranger yourself, weren't you?"

"Was once."

"Ever work together?"

"Some."

"I kind of guessed that, by the way he sided us."

"Yeah."

Kaler looked at him curiously. "That all you got to say about it?"

"What else?"

"I figured you'd owe him thanks."

Kenton said, "He didn't expect none. It was his way of paying back, I reckon."

"Regular buddy, then?"

"Close as I ever been to having one."

"Didn't think you had it in you," Kaler said.

Kenton was strangely thoughtful. "Truth is, I didn't either."

They rode on in silence, each thinking about the incipient rendezvous with the Mexican officials with whom they had made their deal. They were aware that here in Sonora one branch of authorities were sometimes engaged in profit-making schemes that conflicted with the operations of other governmental segments.

It was the land of the *mordida*, "the bite," most often the gain acquired by securing a bribe. More loosely, the term could cover any illicit profit by those in authority.

Kenton and Kaler knew the Sonora officials who offered them a forty-percent commission on the estimated worth of the contraband arms would be selling them somewhere and pocketing the proceeds.

Kaler was curious. "Where the hell do you suppose they sell the guns?"

Kenton said, "In a country like Mexico, you can always sell weapons."

"You reckon they end up in Yaqui hands, after all?"

"Wouldn't surprise me none," Kenton said. "Ain't a concern of ours. A deal like this, the only ones losing are the suppliers up in Tucson."

Kaler was briefly silent again. Then he said, "We could be losers too, if we run onto a bunch of armed Yaquis on the warpath."

"Ain't nothing guaranteed safe," Kenton replied. "But the driver tells me this load was to be delivered to Yaqui representatives east of where we're going."

"We going the same place again?"

"Yeah. Pozo Seco," Kenton said. "Hope the spring ain't dried up again. Desolate damn spot, ain't it? Nothing there but that part-time watering hole."

"Our Mex confederates want to damn sure stay clear of their own customs agents, I guess," Kaler said.

"For sure. And so do we. But another hour and we'll be there."

There was rolling country ahead, and eventually Kenton directed the wagon driver toward a distant shallow canyon. Just a hint of green showed at its mouth, evidence of scant growth of paloverde or such.

"No sign of our friends," Kaler said.

"Taking advantage of what shade there is," Kenton said. "I guess."

They drew closer, and Kaler said, "I don't see a wagon. They're supposed to have their own transport for the load. I don't see horses, and I don't see men."

"What the hell!" Kenton said.

They halted.

"Somebody might have got wise to what we're doing. Maybe stopped our friends or scared them," Kaler said.

The driver came alert as he heard what they were saying.

He spoke up suddenly, "Listen! If your market ain't

here, let's take the weapons over east to where them Yaqui representatives is most likely waiting."

Kenton said, "They got money?"

The driver was silent.

"Well," Kenton said, "have they?"

"I made one delivery before. And, just as now, I was given no mention of collecting money. My understanding is that the suppliers are paid in advance up in Tucson by Yaqui sympathizers there."

Kenton said, "So why would we take the shipment to them?"

"Reckon I ain't too bright in suggesting it to you," the driver said. "I only did so because it was the job I was given to do, I guess." He paused. "That, and I kind of sympathize with them Yaquis myself, the way they been treated."

"Forget it," Kenton said. "I hate the bastards."

The driver shrugged. "It's your call."

Kaler said to Kenton, "Well?"

"We'll push on into the canyon. Could be we just got here early. But keep your eyes open."

"Hell, man," Kaler said, "you don't have to tell me that."

They hesitated at the canyon mouth. The place was deserted.

A short distance in, the spring was dry.

Pozo Seco—Dry Well—was living up to its name.

The few light-green paloverde trees spread a scant shade.

Kaler said, "It ain't much, but compared to the country around here, it has the look of a picnic area."

That's when the bullet hit him in the back and dropped him out of his saddle. He landed hard on the dry-baked earth alongside the wagon.

The driver said, "Goddam!" and remained seated, not moving.

Kenton kicked his mount around and started fast out of the canyon.

The driver cried, "Wait!"

Kenton was already yards away and had his horse into an all-out run.

The driver still did not move. He just sat on the wagon seat and let go with a string of curses.

And then, as he saw the mounted Rurales spew out of the heights on either side of the canyon to take up the chase of the fugitive, his voice turned to one of eager encouragement.

"Get the yellow-livered bastard!" he yelled to them. "Get the son of a bitch!"

Out on the flat, the six-man squad of sombreroed riders was maintaining an equal pace with Kenton, but not gaining on him either.

In their lead was Sergeant Soto. He was quirting his horse, as he was driven himself.

He had recognized Kenton back there in the canyon and was about to take his own action against him, when some fool among his men fired without order at the other American.

By god, he'd take care of that fool when this was over. Maybe make him dig a grave big enough to share with this *maldito* gringo, share his execution too.

Soto quirted the horse again, although he knew it could go no faster. There ahead was the cursed son of a whore who had given him trouble, and who he later learned had killed his black-sheep cousin. So the cousin was a bad one? Blood was blood, kin was kin. And Soto had heard in detail from Sheriff Castillo how the son of a whore had executed his relative.

¡Por Dios! He would pay for what he had done. Soto swore he would see to that.

It was luck that he had been sent to the suspected rendezvous site by Colonel Kosterlitzky after the colonel uncovered the illicit activities of a handful of Sonora officials.

Some other federal squad could have been given the order.

In which case he would not now be closing in on the hated gringo in a race for the border.

Wes Barnes had retraced his way to the Naco road and on up to Bisbee. From there he phoned in a preliminary report to Ryerson.

"You want me to go on up to Tucson to follow up?"

Ryerson did not answer at once. After some thought, he said, "No. I've got a ranger works there regularly. He knows the town like a book. Come on in, and we'll get your information into a detailed report to send him and let him do the legwork up there."

A day and a half later Barnes was back in Douglas.

Together, he and Ryerson spent considerable time getting his information on paper. When they were finished, Cap leaned back in his desk chair. "So Jake has gone mercenary."

"Nothing dishonest about what he's doing, really," Barnes said. "And you've got to hand it to him for guts."

"I'm surprised the Mexicans would deal with him. Their criticism and rage over his actions as a ranger was part of the reason I finally let him go."

Barnes said, "He's dealing with a different branch of officials."

"Not Colonel Kosterlitzky, I guess," Cap said. "And sure as hell not that Rurale sergeant."

"Sergeant Soto?"

"Yeah, Soto," Ryerson said.

The phone on Ryerson's desk rang, and he lifted the receiver.

Sergeant Soto was infuriated that neither he nor any of his squad could overtake the fleeing gringo.

At last he halted his men and sat his saddle, watching in

the distance as his quarry crossed the border and became legally out of his reach.

It was another of the inequities between the adjoining countries.

Since their formation, the rangers had managed to wangle somewhat reluctant permission to enter Mexico if in pursuit.

But the reverse had never been true. The gringos had not let any Rurales cross into Arizona on the trail of escaping Mexican criminals.

So Soto and his squad remained halted as their quarry disappeared, but Soto was thinking.

Thinking that this might be the time to change all that.

When Ryerson picked up the phone, a voice said, "This is Sheriff Robert Castillo, in Nogales."

"Yes, Sheriff."

"Listen, I've had a Rurale Sergeant Soto hanging around here for a couple of days trying to get permission to cross into Arizona after that ex-ranger of yours named Kenton. Says he's involved in an arms-smuggling scheme. They were hot on his heels till the border."

"Kenton, eh? What can I do about it?"

"I'm wondering if you can use your influence to get him permission. After all, Colonel Kosterlitzky has used his to let your rangers enter Mexico."

Ryerson said, "That's because he realizes that doing so helps rid his area of gringo troublemakers."

"Exactly. And granting his men the same permission could help us in the same way."

"Kenton is an American."

"Suppose he was a Mexican, like those two nationals he slaughtered?"

The ranger captain said, "I have brought this up to the governor before, at Kosterlitzky's request. And the answer has always been a flat refusal. In the governor's own words, the Territorial legislature simply would not tolerate such a condition. One of their leaders was quoted as saying, 'What would our citizens say if a squad of Rurales came swarming in after Mexican criminals who've escaped into our sovereignty?' "

"Hardly fair, is it?"

"The governor fears such feelings in the Territorial body could result in the abolishment of the rangers. We have some political opposition among them who cite the operating cost of maintaining us."

"Your answer, then, is no?" Sheriff Castillo said.

"I'm afraid so."

The sheriff slammed down the receiver.

Ryerson said to Barnes, "That was Castillo in Nogales. He informs me that Jake Kenton is wanted for arms-smuggling involvement. And Soto and his Rurales want a permit to cross the border to hunt him. Asked my help with the governor."

Barnes said, "And?"

"You heard me tell him. There's not a chance."

Barnes said, "Jake wasn't exactly smuggling arms."

"Apparently the Rurales see it differently."

"Jake's luck again," Barnes said. "I mean reaching the border. I'm glad he made it."

"Still like him, eh?"

"I never liked him," Barnes said. "But I still feel I owe him." He paused. "And I wish to hell I didn't."

With the border behind him, Kenton could feel safe from Rurale pursuit. He slowed down and made his way northward, angered at losing his potential profit from the arms venture.

CHAPTER 12

TWO THINGS RANKLED Kenton: First, was his discharge from the rangers by Ryerson; second, was Sergeant Soto and his Rurales spoiling his arrangement with the corrupt Sonoran officials.

In both cases, Kenton felt he was, in his own way, combating those who broke the law. And what did it get him?

He was a man who reacted strongly against those who opposed him. And he was also a man who craved excitement.

Days passed as he drifted aimlessly about the Territory, rebellion steadily growing within him.

Along with this grew increasing boredom.

The excitement he had known as a ranger made his present life as a drifter unbearable, which was why he had got involved in the gunrunning scheme when it was broached to him by the shady customs agent, Kaler. The two had met while drinking in one of Bisbee's bars.

Thinking about this now, he felt a strong return of his festering resentment toward Ryerson.

Kenton had got the job done on every assignment given him. For a considerable while Ryerson had tolerated his methods, seeming to go along with Kenton's philosophy that the ends justified the means.

Why the change? It occurred to him then what the captain had said at the time of his dismissal from the force. About how the opposition politicians at the capital were handed big-bore ammunition by what Kenton had done to those two cholo bandits. And that happened because that

119

Sheriff Castillo in Nogales had made trouble for him, daring to take Kenton in and jail him.

Half the Territorial legislature and Castillo also became objects of his resentment.

To top it off, he was without income and almost out of money.

All this ignited a rage in a man who, under the best of circumstances, had a dangerously short fuse.

CHAPTER 13

WEEKS WENT BY as Ryerson sent Barnes out on solo assignments.

One was up in the Chiricahua Mountains, where Barnes went at the request of an Arizona Cattle Growers Association inspector named Shafer. Together they rounded up sixty-five cattle with altered brands. They caught the rustler and got him jailed.

He went next to the Aravaipa Valley to arrest a rancher accused of murder.

Then came an off-beat assignment, hardly part of a ranger's duty.

Ryerson had been contacted by the Indian Agent at the San Carlos Reservation, asking for his testimony to back a request for an increase of the rations issued to the Apaches there.

Cap couldn't make it at this particular time and had sent Barnes as his emissary.

It was an experience Barnes would not forget.

The agent introduced him to several Apache spokesmen. One in particular, who was called Chanz, impressed Barnes when he said, in English, "There be many time when rations do not come. Those time we live on only cactus fruit and acorns we can gather on the mountain."

Barnes told him he would include that in his report, and he did.

They had shaken hands on that promise, but Barnes had heard no more.

One day when Barnes reported in, Ryerson said, "I've got another detective chore for you."

Barnes made no comment. He met the captain's stare and waited.

"Been a series of stage holdups reported over the past weeks," Cap said, "while you've been otherwise occupied."

"Where?"

"Here in Cochise County, mostly. Over in the western part."

"You said a series? You mean by one man?"

"Lone bandit. Descriptions vary, as they usually do, but there is enough similarity to make me think it could be."

"Where do I start?"

Ryerson glanced at the paper on which he had scribbled notes.

"His first strike might have been near Contention. But he's been ranging all over the area, north and south."

"Into Mexico?"

"Haven't heard anything from down there. He's keeping busy enough on this side, I'd guess."

"I'm on my way," Barnes said. "It'll be a change from hunting rustlers."

Ryerson studied his face and appeared about to speak, then changed his mind.

"Something else, Cap?"

Ryerson hesitated, then shook his head. "Just don't be too surprised at what you may turn up."

"What does that mean?"

His answer was another shake of the head, and Cap said, "Good luck."

CHAPTER 14

EX-RANGER JAKE KENTON surprised himself at how easy it had been for him to switch sides from lawman to outlaw.

A fortuitous coincidence launched him into his new line of work. He had stumbled upon a robbery in progress, a stage holdup near Contention, where he happened to be riding at the time. He acted instinctively to thwart it, but after he succeeded he uncharacteristically took the gathered spoils and rode off with them.

He was further surprised at the feeling of satisfaction this had given him.

A satisfaction increased by the astonished reactions of the stage driver and his three passengers as well as that of the wounded bandit who fled the scene, dropping his sack of loot.

Kenton had made one mistake: he'd acted with an uncovered face, although he had been unshaven for a considerable period and his black beard would make identification by strangers difficult.

He was more careful the next time.

A week later a second opportunity presented itself to him.

He had just ridden into Fairbank as a train pulled in. Darkness was falling, but he saw a pair of horsemen make for the express car.

Kenton halted to watch and heard the words flung at the express messenger within, followed by several shots to emphasize their demand to open up.

The messenger apparently refused, and the bandits

blasted the lock away with gunfire, entered, and grabbed up a sack of currency.

At that moment the expressman opened up with a shotgun, killing one bandit as the other shot him in the head and fled with the single bag.

It was dark now, but Kenton followed the bandit as he spurred off. Two hundred yards away, Kenton shot him out of the saddle, dismounted to pick up the currency, and disappeared.

The trainmen and others who converged on the express car were confused by what had taken place.

And Kenton made his escape while they were still pondering.

Again, the amount taken was small, probably an overflow amount from a large shipment ensconced in a safe.

But Kenton was still satisfied. And hell, he told himself, so far he was actually making a career of robbing the robbers.

It wouldn't happen like that often, he knew.

But he found he didn't really care.

Now, he began to think seriously of planning his own robberies.

There was excitement, action, and profit to be had. He could work either side of the border, he thought. It was a lucrative way to play out the hand that had been dealt him.

Barnes followed Ryerson's suggestion and went to the area around the old stamp-mill town of Contention, with its adobe buildings. Over the years a lot of ore had been crushed here, brought up from Tombstone.

A couple of days spent conversing with random residents brought only the remark of one old-timer that there had been a stage robbed nearby, if he recollected correctly.

"Hereabouts somewhere," the oldster said.

"When was that?"

"Been several weeks, I think." There was a pause. "Or was it months maybe?"

"Any particulars?"

"Particulars?" the old resident said. "Now, what would they be? You seen one stage holdup, you seen them all."

"You ever see one?"

"Nope, I never have," the old man said.

That wasn't much to go on, Barnes was thinking.

"But there seems to be an uncommon lot of them going on these days, what I hear."

"Where?"

"Why, all over the place. Don't you read the papers?"

"Seems like I did hear of some," Barnes said. "That's why I was asking."

The oldster was staring at his ranger star, as if he had just noticed it. "I thought, by god, that you might have had a reason."

"Yeah," Barnes said. "Well, thanks anyway."

"Wait a minute! I just remembered. That early holdup I mentioned—it took place up the road a piece, between here and St. David. And it was a odd one, I recall now."

"Odd?"

"The way the driver told it, they was being robbed by this one galoot, when another rode up, shot him in the arm, chasing him off, then picked up the sack of takings the first feller dropped and rode off with it his own self."

"Just like that?"

"Never said a word to nobody, the driver said."

"Any description of him?"

"Black-bearded bastard is all the driver could say. No face covering or anything. Just like he done it all as a afterthought."

Barnes was thoughtful, then said, "I'm glad you remembered about this."

"Hell," the oldster said, "it ain't something a feller would forget, now, is it?"

"Driver anywhere around where I can talk to him?"

"His home station is in St. David, north up the river a piece."

"And his name?"

The old man's face grew blank.

"His name?" Barnes said again.

"I'm thinking on it. I know it as well as my own."

Barnes waited.

There was a long silence before an answer came.

"Raysh Morgan!"

"Raysh?" Barnes said.

"Short for Horatio," the old man said. "Ain't likely a man could forget a name like that, is it?"

"I'll ride up and see him," Barnes said.

He found Morgan at the station, about to make a run northward and with little time to spare in discussion with him.

He was a sunburned, solid chunk of a man, nearing forty, and though poised for departure, he tried to be cordial.

"Yes," he said, "I recall the incident. I've been held up more than once since I took this job driving stage, but unlike them other times, two things stick in my mind. One, of course, is being robbed by the man me and the passengers thought was saving our bacon, as somebody apparently already told you.

"And the other was that, although I only got maybe one good look at his face, there seemed something familiar there, like I maybe seen him someplace before, though I couldn't be sure. I still have that feeling when I think about it. But I never yet been able to place where or when that could be." He paused. "Of course I been in a lot of Arizona towns before I took his job earlier in the year. I could have seen him most anywhere in a crowd or someplace. I ain't sure even about that. Maybe I never did."

"It's something I'll consider," Barnes said.

"Yeah," Morgan said. "Sorry I can't spend more time with you, but I got a schedule to keep."

"Thanks, anyway."

"This jehuing is a tough life," Morgan said. "Sometimes I think I was better off working in the mines at Morenci."

He clambered up to the driver's seat, tossed the reins, and got the team moving in a cloud of dust.

Morenci, Barnes thought. He wondered if the jehu was one of those who had left during the strike threat.

Driving stagecoach was a hard life, he supposed, but it had to be better than that of a miner.

Just before he pulled away, Morgan called, "There was some talk later, after the express-car robbery at Fairbank, that the one who robbed us might have had a part in that one too."

He was gone then, too late for Barnes to question him further.

Barnes cursed silently, then shrugged.

A little later he mounted up and turned south toward the railroad town Morgan had mentioned.

In Fairbank, he looked up the town's newspaper office.

The Fairbank Clarion was a poor second to the *Tombstone Epitaph*, but he supposed it took as great an interest in local happenings as did its prestigious rival centered miles to the east.

Its editor and printer came out of the rear pressroom when he heard the bell on the door signal Barnes's entry.

Barnes had seen many of his calling and was struck by the aura some printers projected—a mixture of ink-stained laborer and lofty pedant.

He recognized it here.

"I'm Samuel Whipple, publisher," the printer said.

"Wes Barnes."

The printer had noted Barnes's star and said, "At your service, Mr. Barnes."

"I'd like to see a back copy of your paper. It concerns a railway express robbery. Maybe I should say an attempted robbery. It took place right here in town."

"Been only one in recent months. How far back are you speaking of?"

"The one you mention could be it," Barnes said.

Whipple went over to an adjoining room and began searching through the papers stacked on its shelves.

Within a few minutes he returned and spread on the counter in front of Barnes an issue bearing a headline referring to the robbery.

"This sound like what you're looking for?"

"I think so," Barnes said.

There was a two-column spread on the front page, and he read through it carefully as the printer returned to the pressroom.

He was going over it in his mind when Whipple came back out.

"That help you any?"

Barnes looked up at him. "Help me with what?" he said.

"You're a ranger, aren't you? I assume you're interested in the rider who got away with the sack of currency."

"I am."

"Like the story says, he was no more than a bystander when the expressman and the one bandit were killing each other. The surviving one was making his getaway when he was shot by the mysterious stranger."

"No identification?" Barnes said.

"Of the stranger? No. But the pair of dead hard cases were known. Both had records and had done time in Yuma Territorial."

"The stranger's escape was witnessed by a few people on the scene, who described his action. But nobody seems to have described *him*," Barnes said.

"It was near dark by then, hard to see. Man appeared to be a white man with a dark growth of beard. Nothing else to go on."

"I see," Barnes said. He paused. "You think he might have been the same one who robbed the St. David stage the week before?"

"You know about that? Must have heard of the speculation some folks engaged in. Well, I wouldn't discount it exactly. But more than likely the similarity of the two actions was just coincidence."

Barnes folded the newspaper and pushed it toward the printer.

"Much obliged," he said.

"Hold on!" the printer said. He stepped over to a short stack of papers at the end of the counter and came back to hand one to Barnes.

"Today's issue," he said. "Mention of a robbery two days ago, down Charleston way."

Barnes opened to the story.

It was a brief account, possibly phoned in to the *Clarion* from a source in the area.

The local bank had been held up by a masked gunman just before noon on the date given. He had no accomplices and had taken by threat a couple of hundred dollars from the lone teller shortly after the bank owner left for lunch.

The robber had then knocked the teller unconscious.

An exchange of gunfire alerted the patrons of the nearby restaurant, including the banker. They rushed to look out on the street, in time to see a man lying beside his hitched horse in front of the bank and another rider disappearing from town.

The downed man was dead. The recovering teller identified him as the robber, but the two hundred dollars was gone.

Barnes looked up from the account, frowning.

The printer said, "That ring a bell with you?"

Barnes was silent, still thinking.

"I got to admit," the printer said, "that even though I composed the story, it never dawned on me till now that we maybe got three of a kind here. Same *modus operandi*."

Barnes stared at him, half irritated at his show-off use of big words, but guessing what they meant.

Whipple must have sensed this, because he said, "I mean there's the same method of operation here—robbing the robber."

"Yeah," Barnes said.

"It doesn't mean he's necessarily doing this every time. Just when the cards fall that way."

"Yeah."

"Kind of strange, I'd say."

"Me too," Barnes said. "I'm much obliged. I'll be heading down that way."

The town had once been a lively stamp-mill center for a Tombstone mining company. On the banks of the San Pedro River, it was marked by a scattering of cottonwoods and weathered structures from the 1880s. Its heyday was long past.

Barnes rode the main street, found the constable's office, and tied up in front of it.

As he entered, the middle-aged local lawman looked up from a battered desk. When he saw Barnes's ranger badge, he stood up and extended his hand.

"Constable Will Divens," he said.

"Ranger Wes Barnes."

Divens gestured to a straight-backed chair and sank back into his own.

Barnes said, "I'm checking into the bank robbery of a couple days ago. Heard about it up at Fairbank."

Divens nodded. "I phoned the report in myself."

"I read the news account up there. You make any attempt to catch the man who took the money?"

"I managed to get a posse together, but we lost the trail a few miles out. None of us is much good at tracking."

"What do you make of it?" Barnes said.

"Hard to figure," Divens said. "I had a dodger on the one who took the money from the teller. Name of Rufus Coldiron. Two-bit badman."

"Yeah?"

"Only thing I can figure is the one that killed him and took the loot was maybe a partner with a grudge. Might have been over a gambling debt or something."

Barnes considered this.

"What do you think?" the constable said.

"You may be right," Barnes said. "Which way was he headed when he left town?"

"Rode out of here southward. Same direction till we lost his tracks. Probably heading for the border."

"I reckon I'll take the trail the same direction," Barnes said, heading for the door.

Constable Divens followed him, eyeing Barnes's horse as he mounted. His eyes rested on the Winchester carbine shoved into its scabbard, the stock and lever protruding for easy grasp.

"Hold on a minute," he said. "I'm noticing that box magazine under the frame of your saddle gun."

"Yeah," Barnes said. "Regulation rifle for us rangers. Eighteen ninety-five model."

"One bit that might identify the killer," Divens said. "We got a gunsmith's shop at the end of the street and he saw the rider passing by when he rushed to look outside after the shooting.

"Being what he is, he noticed the scabbard gun the stranger carried. I recall his mentioning that box magazine model."

"Lots of them in use," Barnes said. "Great weapon."

"Must be," the constable said, "if they picked them for you rangers."

"Yeah," Barnes said, and kicked his heels to the horse.

CHAPTER 15

HE HAD RIDDEN only a few miles when he came to a roadside saloon; he would have passed it by, had he not seen a horse, hitched among others, that happened to catch his eye.

And likely wouldn't have, had he not at that moment been thinking of Constable Divens's remark about the bank robber's Winchester '95.

The horse's near side was facing his approach and revealed that model of saddle gun.

Which meant nothing, really. As he had told the constable, there were quite a lot of them in use.

Still, he decided to go in.

There were several patrons, a couple at the bar, others at random tables. A quick glance showed him only strangers, so he went to the bar and ordered a beer from the man behind it.

"Busy morning?" Barnes said.

The barkeep said, "Not bad for this time of a weekday." He found some work to do farther down the bar, after a brief glance at Barnes's badge.

Could mean something about the class of his customers, Barnes thought. But not necessarily so.

The barkeep's attitude was enough to irritate him, and he said, "Seven horses outside and only six customers."

"One's out back in the privy."

Even as he spoke there was the sound of a rear door slamming and footsteps coming through a narrow hallway.

He turned to face that direction just as Kenton appeared.

Barnes's face showed concern at seeing him.

When Kenton saw Barnes, he looked momentarily startled; his steps slowed for a second, then, regaining his composure, he strode toward him.

He spoke effusively, but did not extend his hand. "What're you doing around here?"

"On assignment," Barnes said.

Kenton said to the barkeep, "Give him another beer. Whiskey for me."

As the barman served them, Kenton said, "What's the assignment?"

"I was looking into the robbery of the Charleston bank."

"Any luck?"

"No," Barnes said. He paused. "What's with you?"

"Worked a while on a ranch."

"You quit?"

"Yeah. Too dull for me."

"You always craved excitement."

"Been gambling some."

"I didn't know you were that good at poker."

"Hell, man, there's other games than poker. I hit a lucky streak now and then."

Barnes was silent.

"So what about this robbery?" Kenton said.

"Have you heard about it?"

"Yeah, I heard mention. Any suspects?"

"None specifically. The one who robbed the bank teller was robbed himself. Shot and killed in front of the bank by another man who rode off."

"So I heard," Kenton said.

"He's the one I'm interested in."

"Why?" Kenton said. "In a way he did the law a favor. Killed a criminal for you, didn't he?"

"Took the bank's money. That's the crime."

"Small sum, wasn't it?"

"Couple of hundred dollars."

"Cheap price for ridding the Territory of an outlaw," Kenton said.

"You're missing the point, Jake."

Kenton did not answer at once. Then he said, "I'm not missing your point—I'm just arguing it."

"Is it important enough for you to argue it?"

"It's my feeling, is all. But hell, forget it. Why should I care?"

"I'm wondering that myself."

"Just a feeling I have. Comes from fighting outlaws myself, I guess."

"Killing them," Barnes said, not knowing quite why he said it.

"Exactly," Kenton said. "The one who killed Rufe Coldiron did what I'd have done in the old days."

"There were two similar cases recently," Barnes said. "Stage holdup near Contention. Railroad express car at Fairbank. You know about them?"

"I heard . . ."

"There's some belief that the same man was involved."

"I heard that too."

"What do you say to that?"

There was a long silence before Kenton spoke. When he did, his words were hard and flat. "What I say, old partner, is to get off his trail."

"Is that a warning?" Barnes said. "Or a threat?"

"It's just sound advice," Kenton said. "So far the man has picked only on outlaws. Don't make him start on lawmen."

"Meaning me?"

"Meaning you," Kenton said. "Will you have another drink before I leave?"

"Where are you heading?"

"South of the border," Kenton said. "I got in mind another business proposition down there."

"Last I knew you got out of there with Soto's squad of Rurales one jump behind you."

"I don't figure to get caught down there. What I got in mind is an in-and-out proposition."

Barnes called in and reported to Ryerson what he'd learned and what he had come to suspect.

"What evidence have we got to bring him in?" Ryerson asked.

"None at this time it looks like," Barnes said. "You want me to try to keep him under surveillance? I think he's headed for Sonora."

"Come in. I've another job for you. We'll let that one ride awhile." He paused. "I half-suspected Jake could be going bad."

"You didn't tell me that when you sent me out," Barnes said.

"I damn near did," Cap said. "But then I was sure you'd balk at the assignment, knowing the experiences you'd shared as partners."

Barnes was silent. He knew this was so.

Cap said, "I'm sending you up north to the Globe area. There's been an outbreak of rustling and robbery in recent weeks."

Barnes said, "How bad?"

"Bad enough, seeing the location has been quiet until now." Ryerson paused. "And bad enough for us to suspect it's a gang operation."

"Any knowledge of their identity?"

"Some. There's been a rumor they're led by an Oklahoma refugee named Trask. Maybe a half dozen in the gang."

"Trask? I don't think I've heard of him."

"Another new arrival from outside the Territory," Ryerson said. "Jud Trask. Said to claim he once rode, as a youngster, with the Daltons."

"Long way from home."

"So are half the outlaws we've been battling against," Ryerson said. "Or hadn't you noticed?"

Barnes did not answer for a moment. Then he said, "Some. But, for me, lately it seems like it's been mostly locals and border jumpers."

"Luck of the draw," Cap said. "But here's your chance for a possible change of experience. That Oklahoma country has bred some of the bloodiest bastards in the history of the West. You could learn how much of it rubbed off on this Trask bunch."

Barnes was silent, thinking about it.

Ryerson then said an unexpected thing. "Here is where Kenton might have been useful to us."

"I don't need his kind."

"I know that. No offense intended. It was just a thought."

Just a thought. But it griped Barnes somehow. As if Cap had second thoughts about sending him up there on his own.

"When do I leave?" he said.

"Now is as good a time as any," Ryerson said.

Barnes, with his horse, debarked from the branch railroad that ran north from the S.P. main line to connect the now-booming mining town of Globe.

North of the town rose the Apache Mountains, to the southwest were the Pinals, which they had skirted on the way. Neither range was familiar to him, a fact that wouldn't make his assignment any easier. He realized that Ryerson, always shorthanded, was forced to use his men as needed, tempered by availability.

He wondered how well the Trask bunch from Oklahoma knew the surrounding country.

The main thoroughfare, Broad Street, wound alongside a creek through a canyon dividing the foothills on which the dwellings of the town were built. On a hillside at the northern limits were the work buildings and the slag and tailing dumps of the famous copper-producing Old Dominion Mine.

As he saddled his mount and rode up Broad, he studied the mix of loitering men in front of the shops and saloons. Mining men, off shift, he supposed. Some cowboys in from neighboring ranches, although he guessed that come Saturday he'd see far more. And a few Apaches from the nearby San Carlos reservation.

The Apaches were mostly in Western range garb, but there was something distinctive about the way they wore it that seemed to set them apart.

It was the others, the gringos, that mostly lured his attention. Could it be possible that there were Trask cohorts among them? A man or two mingling and gathering information on likely targets for outlaw gain? Payroll shipments, cattle buyer or seller deals, outlying ranches with far-grazing cattle to be easily rustled? A bank or two with periodic large deposits?

According to Ryerson, any or all of these were fields in which the Trask bunch were, or could be, suspect.

And where the hell did they hide out?

He put up his mount at a livery and took a room at the Hotel Dominion nearby. The old desk clerk eyed him closely as he was signing in.

Barnes noticed and said, "Something bothering you, fellow?"

He had put his badge in his pocket before he got off the train, but the clerk said, "Ranger, ain't you, sir? I recall seeing you at Douglas."

"Forget you did," Barnes said.

"As you wish, sir," the clerk said. "Would you be here on account of the hell the Trask bunch been raising lately?"

"Always interested in hell-raisers," Barnes said. "What do you know about them?"

"Mostly rumors. They been getting credit for near every

crime been committed around here. Mostly, I guess, because Trask got hisself drunk one time and boasted he'd
rode with the Daltons."

"He still bragging about it?"

"Nobody's seen him in town here since. Knowed he
made a fool mistake mouthing off like that, I reckon."

"No sight of him?"

"Not personal. But two of his men who'd been with him
that time was recognized last week by Jesse Crump, owns
the hardware store. Came in big as life, held him up,
robbed his till and took most of the guns he had in his
display rack, and rode off again."

"Where do they hole up between jobs?"

"I don't rightly know. You want to question Crump, his
place is a couple blocks up the street. You'll see his name
on his sign."

"Thanks," Barnes said. "I will. But, as a favor, keep your
mouth shut about me."

"Be glad to oblige, Ranger," the clerk said, his tone too
sincere to be believed.

Barnes found Crump standing in the doorway of his
store. He was exchanging words with a range-garbed
Apache who was sitting on the edge of his porch.

Both men looked up as he approached.

"Mr. Crump?" Barnes said, ignoring the Indian.

"That's me."

Barnes took out his badge and showed it. "Ranger
Barnes."

"Barnes." Crump gave him a short nod. "What can I do
for you?"

"Heard you were robbed."

"Yeah, I was. A couple of weeks ago."

"Guns and cash," Barnes said.

"You've been talking to somebody."

"You know the men who did it?"

"Not personally. But I'd seen them once before, when

they were likkered up here in town with the one called Trask."

"Two of the Jud Trask bunch, then?"

"I'm sure of it."

"I was sent here to run them down."

"One ranger?"

"We're spread thin, Mr. Crump. I was hoping to get a posse together to help."

"You're a little late for that."

"I mean if I can first find out where they are."

Barnes sensed some movement in the position of the Apache and turned quickly to look. The Apache was standing now, facing him, and their eyes met and held. He was about Barnes's age.

A long moment went by before recognition came to Barnes.

"It been a long time," the Apache said. "You remember me?"

"Chanz! Isn't it?"

"Yes, *Nantan.*"

"Not *Nantan,*" Barnes said. "Just Barnes."

Chanz smiled.

"How are things, Chanz?"

"Better now. More ration since you come to see how it was with us Apache at San Carlos."

Barnes thought, Could it be my report, relayed by Ryerson, did some good? If any good came of it, it was because the captain had endorsed it. It was Cap's testimony the Indian agent had wanted.

He said, "I'm glad."

"And now," the Apache said, "I hear what you say to store man. Me, too, see them men, also see other drunk time. You want to find?"

"Yes."

"I help, because what you done."

"You know where they are?"

"Them and all bunch hide in Pinal Mountains. Some Apaches know, tell me. I try tell to some whites, they don't listen. You listen?"

"I listen. You know the Pinals?"

"I been there sometime. You rent horse for me, I go with you."

"Will do!"

"Maybe gun, too? We been go after bad men, right?"

"Gun, too," Barnes said. "You betcha." He felt trust in Chanz.

It was evening when they left. Barnes had rented a horse, laid in supplies in their saddlebags for four days of scant rations, and bought a used but serviceable Krag carbine for the Apache.

He also canceled his hotel accommodations after eliciting from Crump all the information about the Trask bunch that was currently known in the Globe area.

They put a lot of miles on the trail toward the Pinals before they made a cold camp that night.

At first light they were on their way again, the Pinals still in the distance, but looming large.

Hours later they reached the rising contours of the range.

They cut into a canyon with trail sign along its sandy bottom. They rode several miles before they came to a ledge that led up the canyon side to a high-rising escarpment. There were scattered pines here, but southeast of the shoulder was a badland mix of rocky draws spotted with catclaw and cactus.

Barnes followed where the Apache led. He seemed to know where he was going, and Barnes, seeing the trace of a used trail, was not concerned.

There was a high sharp peak rising ahead, and Barnes wondered if that was the trail's destination.

As he pondered this their path veered north so abruptly as to almost reverse their direction.

"You've been this way before?" he said.

"Yes. I hunt here few year back. I try remember now, think this trail go to place of spring maybe. Good place for bad men to make camp," Chanz said.

Barnes thought about this.

The Apache said then, "You ready fight all bunch alone?"

"No. I want only to find where they're at. I'll get a posse together before I try to make an arrest."

"When we find," the Apache said, "better we shoot dead first. Then arrest."

His words put Barnes in mind of Kenton.

The thought brought with it a fleeting wish that Jake were here with him. He recalled that Ryerson had hinted a similar feeling when he'd sent him on the assignment.

He shook off the wish now, angry even at the idea.

Still . . .

"We getting close, I think," Chanz said.

But it seemed he was wrong.

Because the trail continued.

It was afternoon now, and the sun had passed above the peaks and rough ridges of the Pinal summits, which the trail's turning had avoided.

Suddenly the Apache halted. Just ahead was a stand of pine.

"Other side trees," he said, "little valley with spring and grass."

"I've got to see the men," Barnes said.

"Tie horses. Best we go on foot."

Barnes debated the risk of leaving the mounts. Suppose they had to run for it?

Chanz noted his hesitation. "You want get close, horse make noise. No good."

Barnes said, "Yeah," and reluctantly tied his horse to one of the pines. The Apache did likewise.

He made no noise when he walked, even though he wore boots.

Barnes tried to do likewise. The cushion of fallen pine needles helped.

They reached the edge of the trees, and just below them lay a sizable meadow of forage grass with a small creek crossing it. Three army-issue tents were pitched near the creek, and horses grazed. A rough stone cooking pit with a metal cover was visible, as were a crudely built table and benches as well as a scatter of riding tack and saddles on improvised racks.

The place had the look of having been used for several months.

Likely since the time Trask had arrived from Oklahoma, Barnes thought.

Three men sat at the table, one of them dealing cards. All were wearing holstered guns.

Chanz touched Barnes's shoulder and pointed them out.

He said, "The one got red hair on face, he Trask. Them other, they robber."

"The ones that robbed Crump?"

"That them two."

"I heard there were five or six in the bunch," Barnes said.

"Maybe so. Maybe in tents."

"Too many to arrest alone," Barnes said.

"I help."

"Even so."

"Why you don't shoot them three from here?"

"That's murder. I'd have to give them a chance to give up first."

"That crazy," the Apache said.

"That's the way it is," Barnes said.

"White man law crazy."

At that moment another man came from one of the tents.

Barnes studied him as he approached those at the table; he wore a revolver too.

"Maybe that's all," Barnes said. He made a change of decision then, and called out, "Trask, drop your weapons!"

All four outlaws drew their guns, looking at the stand of pines from where his voice had come.

Finally Trask yelled, "Who the hell are you?"

"Arizona Rangers," Barnes answered, stretching the truth to include Chanz.

There was silence and no movement from the men at the table, still holding their handguns at the ready.

"Drop them I said!"

"Goddamn!" Trask said, still not obeying.

"You want a .30-.40 bullet through your chest?" Barnes called. "You got thirty seconds!"

Trask cursed again and lowered his weapon as if to drop it.

And at that moment a voice behind Barnes yelled, "Drop your own!"

Barnes whirled, Winchester leveled, and triggered off a shot that hit the man who held a Colt, hit him with a bullet through the gut.

The man, dressed in range garb like Trask and the others, looked up at him with dying eyes and said inanely, "I seen your horses, and sneaked up." Said like he was bragging about it.

Barnes called down to Trask then, "I just shot one of your men up here! Give up or you'll get the same."

But the Trask men held their weapons and were running for the nearby cover of a boulder-dotted hillock.

Barnes and Chanz both fired. The Apache missed, but Barnes's shot took Trask in the leg, and he fell.

One of the others kept running, but two turned back

and grabbed Trask by either arm and began dragging him
toward cover.

Barnes could have shot any one of the three, but he hesitated, surprised at the action of the pair. They were the
ones who'd robbed Crump. You didn't often see that kind
of loyalty among the outlaw kind.

Even as he hesitated, the Apache fired and dropped one
of them. The other tried to tug Trask alone, but the weight
was too much after a couple of yards.

Barnes swerved his aim and caught the running man just
as he reached the rocky part of the hillock.

He came rolling down the side of it, then lay still.

The man still at the fallen Trask's side let go of his arm
and raised both hands high.

"It's your win!" he yelled.

Trask moved then, his hand groping out as if searching
for the handgun he'd clung to even as they dragged him,
but had lost when his arm was dropped.

The surrendering outlaw kicked the gun out of his
reach and said, "No, goddammit!"

And it was over.

The outlaw in the pines and the one at the hillock were
dead.

Trask had a severe leg wound, as did the one that the
Apache had dropped.

The outlaws' horses were caught and saddled, bodies
slung across two of them. The wounded were helped to
mount and their wrists lashed to the saddle horns.

Barnes manacled the unwounded outlaw, but left him
awkwardly able to rein, and with the threat of a bullet if he
tried to flee.

The spare horses in the meadow were let loose to roam.

Barnes and the Apache led the wounded and the dead
back to Globe.

Another assignment done, Barnes thought.

CHAPTER 16

JAKE KENTON KNEW where he was going. From his tour as a mine guard at Cananea he recalled there was a little town called Morelos near the last dry reach of the San Pedro River, a dozen miles below the Mexican border.

He remembered it had a bank that handled deposits for some American mining ventures in the area. A branch of the *Banco de Méjico.*

After his conversation with Barnes, he was certain he was under suspicion of having a part in the discussed robberies. It would be wise, he thought, to avoid any more activity in the Territory until ranger interest in him dissipated a little.

The thought of robbing a Mexican bank intrigued him.

It could be exciting—and profitable. The small hauls he'd made on his first three crimes were scarcely worth his involvement, he thought. Penny-ante stuff.

There could damn well be a bigger stake potential down there.

And taking from a Mexican bank was easy enough on his conscience. Mexicans had given him enough trouble in the past.

It was Toriano, Sergeant Soto's trusted corporal, who saw from a distance the horseman cross from the American side.

The Rurales had been patrolling the border vicinity while Colonel Kosterlitzky once again pressured Arizona officials to allow them to cross the line in pursuit of criminals escaping to Arizona sanctuary.

145

Apparently the colonel had hopes now, Soto was thinking, and his guess was that a squad, preferably his own, might be kept on this duty. That would please Soto. He hated border jumpers—both those who escaped him by going north and those who came south to commit crimes in his territory.

As he was made aware of the rider, he sent Toriano, who had the best eyes of his squad, to approach unseen to try to identify him. Some of these border jumpers were known to the Rurales.

They were in an area of occasional knolls, so Toriano was able to do this and was back soon.

"Well?" Sergeant Soto said.

"He is our old *enemigo*," Toriano said. "The one who was once a ranger. The one who is now an outlaw for smuggling guns."

"Kenton!"

"The same, *jefe*. But why does he enter our country again?"

Soto said, "To commit another crime most likely."

"Will we take him in, *jefe*?"

"We will see what he is up to that is new," Soto said. "Those old charges about the gun smuggling to the Yaquis might now be hard to prove. Too many Sonora state officials involved."

"I understand," Toriano said. "And in this hilly country I can track him unnoticed." He paused. "Perhaps he is riding to Morelos."

"That will make your tracking easier," Soto said.

"But what is in Morelos to attract him, *jefe*?"

"There is a bank in Morelos," Soto said, after some thought.

Kenton paused outside the town to case the bank's surroundings.

It was an isolated spot for a bank, as he had remembered.

But it was on the Mexican Railway lines connecting Cananea, Nogales, and Naco by a winding route that made it convenient for shipping the needs of the area mines, which included payroll deposits in U.S. currency for those with American workers. He knew that from when he worked at Cananea.

As he scrutinized the town, he saw nothing to deter him. He saw no office of a local law officer, although he supposed there might be one among the adobe buildings.

He was not too worried about the local law anyway. Probably fat and lazy, he thought, and not too brave with a fancy pistol in an ornate holster.

He rode up to the bank and slip hitched his horse at the rack for a quick getaway.

Soto halted his men forty yards away as they came to the end of a coulee, and watched the ex-ranger's action.

"We could shoot him from here," Toriano said.

"Let him rob the bank," Soto said. "Then we will have an airtight case against him."

"He is a dangerous man, *jefe*."

"There are six of us here today," Soto said, looking across the wide dirt roadway as Kenton entered the bank. "There is one of him."

Toriano was silent. He sometimes made suggestions, but he knew better than to argue.

They watched as Kenton dismounted and entered the bank.

Time went by.

Toriano, who was of an impatient nature, began to fidget.

"Steady," Soto said.

"Suppose he shoots someone inside?" Toriano said. "Is your plan to wait worth that risk?"

"It is to me," Soto said. "But if we hear a shot we will rush the place."

His words did not seem to relieve the corporal.

"He is a long while in there," Toriano said.

"He is gathering much loot, perhaps."

"The brush here hides us," Toriano said. "But it will not stop bullets. And I keep remembering the description of how he killed the four gringo rustlers in the cantina at Cocóspera."

'We will beat him to his weapon draw."

"But at Cocóspera they say he—"

"Enough," Soto said. "I will say when."

And at that moment, Kenton came out, carrying a filled sack, and one of the Rurales, keyed-up by the wait, fired a shot that missed.

"Now!" Soto said.

Almost simultaneously, Kenton dropped the sack, drew his revolver, and got off two quick shots into the brushy draw.

One struck Soto in the shoulder, and he dropped his gun. Another took Toriano in the chest.

As Toriano fell, he murmured, "Like at Cocóspera, *jefe*, . . ."

Soto knew then he had made a mistake. One that had lost him his most trusted aide.

He bent down, fumbling to grasp his fallen weapon, and found his fingers would not work.

The other four men were firing at Kenton. They missed, but Kenton didn't. He returned fire with two more wounding shots.

His horse took a grazing bullet across its near haunch that sent it jerking away from his boot as he tried for a stirrup. As Kenton stepped toward it, he saved himself from a passing bullet that knocked out a window of the bank. He toed into the stirrup and hauled into the saddle as two of the Rurales continued to fire.

And then he was racing away down the dirt road—without the sack of money. He had not tried to retrieve it, uncertain of the damage his brush shots had done.

Kenton swore at his luck.

Soto was swearing at his own luck. His shoulder wound was bleeding badly, and the pain had totally disabled his arm.

The conditions of his two wounded men were less serious, but they were in no shape to pursue the escaping gringo.

Toriano was dead. That left two abled-bodied Rurales, and they were needed to help those hurt.

One of them asked, "Will we follow the son of a whore, *jefe?*"

Soto shook his head.

He was staring at the door of the bank from which a half dozen employees came rushing.

He stepped out onto the roadway, followed by the others, and halted, waiting.

The man in the lead reached him and said, "Is he gone?"

"Gone," Sergeant Soto said.

The banker stared at his wound and at the wounds of the others.

"We need medical attention," Soto said. "Can it be had here?"

"No, *sargento*. Not here."

Soto was silent. His pain was great. As was that of his wounded men, although they struggled not to show it before these soft-handed bank employees.

"But you are in luck," the bank manager said. "There is a train due to return from hauling supplies to Cananea. It will be passing through to go back to Nogales."

"When?"

"It is overdue."

"Stop it, you hear?"

"Of course. And there will be an empty freight car or

two, into which you can load your horses. Perhaps a two-hour ride, señor."

Soto swore under his breath.

"That gringo, he was some *pistolero*!" the banker said. "Three out of five wounded!"

"And one dead," an unwounded Rurale said.

"One dead?"

"Shall I drag Toriano from the brush, *jefe*?" the Rurale said.

The pain on Soto's face was abruptly erased by rage.

"Drag him? No! Carry him! And with respect!"

"Come into the bank," the manager said. "And we will give you what first aid we can, while you await the train."

They all moved toward the bank, a couple of the employees leading horses to the hitchrack.

The dropped money sack had already been taken inside.

At least he and his men had prevented the whore's son gringo from getting away with it, Soto thought.

But this was one more act by the ex-ranger that demanded retribution.

More than that, Toriano's death had now launched Soto on a personal vendetta.

Kenton raced his horse to the river before he halted to look back. He was surprised to see no pursuers.

But that did not mean they wouldn't be coming. During the fast shoot-out he had glimpsed the tall peaked sombreros worn by the Rurales, and the garb of one who he was almost certain was Sergeant Soto.

That was the first one he might have hit. One who had gone down from sight, as had the second. How badly were they hurt, if at all?

He had no way of knowing, but slowed his pace to save his horse, deciding to keep an eye on his backtrail and stay ready to sprint if he had to.

He swore now, aloud and long to relieve his feelings.

Soto again? If it was, the frequency of their encounters was disconcerting. He had grown to hate the bastard.

He hoped his bullet back there had killed him.

Hell, he hoped that, no matter who it was. They were enemy, weren't they?

He followed the river back toward the border.

Empty handed.

His frustration grew.

Captain Ryerson picked up the receiver of his ringing phone at headquarters in Douglas.

"Arizona Rangers. Captain Ryerson here."

A torrent of words answered him.

"Slow down, Sheriff," Ryerson said. When Castillo was aroused, a trace of accent from his family upbringing flavored his words.

"Who? Kenton?"

"Down in Morelos. Shot up a squad of Rurales. Tried to rob the bank there."

"In Morelos," Ryerson said. "What do you want from me?"

"Listen, one of the wounded was Sergeant Soto."

"Soto?"

"Listen," Castillo said, "he also wounded two others. And killed Corporal Toriano."

Ryerson was silent.

"You hear what I say?" Castillo said. "One dead and three wounded."

"Where are they?"

"Medically treated in Nogales across the line in Mexico."

"Sorry to hear this happened," Ryerson said. "I mean that."

"Captain, this time you've got to do something."

Ryerson was silent again. He did not like other lawmen telling him what he had to do.

"Listen," Castillo said, "Kosterlitzky is writing to the governor about this. You'll get no more cooperation from him until you put Kenton behind bars. Or better yet, shoot the son of a bitch."

This time Ryerson's hesitation was brief. "I'll get out a warrant for his arrest."

"By god, you'd better," Castillo said.

Ryerson started to slam the receiver onto the hook before he got any more unwanted advice from the Santa Cruz County sheriff. He caught himself in time, and said, "Give me the details of what went on down there."

Castillo did so.

When he'd finished, Ryerson said, "So he didn't get away with any money." He was thinking of what Kenton might be trying next this side of the border.

Castillo did not answer at once. When he did, he spoke in an offended tone.

"Hell, man, we don't want him charged with attempted robbery. The charge will be murder. Or doesn't the killing of a *Mexican* officer constitute murder in your book?"

"I didn't mean that," Ryerson said. "I was thinking of something else when I said it."

Then, because Castillo's words had a delayed irritation for him, he said, "Anything Kenton commits in Santa Cruz County is also a top priority for your own efforts. You're the sheriff there."

Castillo said, "I had him jailed once, and you're the one who got him free."

"He was a ranger then," Ryerson said. "What he did, he did in what he thought was his line of duty. He was wrong about it and paid for it by being discharged."

"That wasn't enough," Castillo said. "I hope you can see that now." He paused, then said, "If he shows up in my county, you can believe he'll get top priority from me. With a vengeance!"

With that, he hung up.

*   *   *

Ryerson immediately sent out orders to all of his men he could contact to be on the alert for Kenton.

For some he would have to wait until they called in from assignments they were on, frequently out in the back-country.

Others of his twenty-six rangers were posted in distant spots where it wasn't likely Kenton would be—spots like Yuma on the California border, Fredonia on Arizona's northern boundary, and not quite that far north at Flagstaff, Williams, and Juniper along the Santa Fe Railroad.

Still, you never could tell about Kenton, Ryerson thought. The man seemed to act on impulse a great deal of the time.

In Nogales, Mexico, just across the border from Nogales, Arizona, Sergeant Soto and his shot-up squad of Rurales had debarked from the train, bearing the body of Toriano. They were quickly escorted by sympathetic citizens to the local hospital.

There, their wounds were treated and the dead man was picked up by an undertaker to be readied for burial.

Soto immediately contacted Kosterlitzky at Magdalena to report the incident at the bank, slanting his version as much as he could to excuse his dead and wounded casualties.

It was something hard to do and was received by the Rurale commander with obvious skepticism mixed with his overriding anger.

The burial of Toriano took place the next day, attended by his comrades.

Soto, his arm in a sling to ease the pain of the bullet-torn tissue and muscles on his shoulder, stood hard-faced and ramrod straight at the graveside as a local priest gave a eulogy.

The priest, who knew none of them, including the deceased, then looked at Soto.

"You wish to say a word, *sargento*?"

"Yes," Soto said.

He paused, and the priest waited politely in his cassock.

"Toriano," Soto said then, "I am going to kill that gringo *bastardo*."

Kenton had crossed the border with conflicting emotions.

I must have knocked the hell out of them, he thought, briefly pleased.

But only briefly. Nothing else had gone right for him. Most of all he was irked at himself for dropping the money sack. It would have been a good haul.

It would have been enough to subsist on for a long time without being concerned about a livelihood.

He was surprised that his interest in money seemed to be partly replacing his interest in exciting action.

Was he suddenly getting old? Money had not been a primary concern in his life until now. Maybe it was the fact that he realized he was under suspicion by Barnes, and undoubtedly by Ryerson, that he was thinking of one big haul and an extensive retirement. Up north, maybe. Thinking about it, he drifted in that direction.

CHAPTER 17

BARNES REPORTED THE demise of the Trask bunch to Ryerson by phone.

He was somewhat disappointed by the captain's reception of the news.

After a brief "Good job. Well done," Ryerson said, "Come in. I want you to hunt up Kenton again."

"Why?"

"He got in a shooting scrape below the border a few days ago. Wounded Sergeant Soto and two of his Rurales, and killed another." The captain hurriedly repeated what Castillo had earlier told him. "Made it back across the line." He paused. "We've got to find him."

Two days later, Barnes reached headquarters. On the way, he felt a growing reluctance for what might lie ahead.

Ryerson seemed to sense this. After a moment of silent staring between them, he said, "It's worse now, Wes."

"Worse? How?"

"He's gone up to Willcox and robbed a bank there. Five thousand dollars in currency and a small amount in gold coins."

"Another robbery," Barnes said.

"And murder," Ryerson said. "He shot to death four of the bank employees when one of them opened fire on him as he was leaving."

"God!" Barnes said. "That's Jake in a gunfight—no mercy!"

"He's got to be stopped."

Barnes was silent.

"A fast-formed civilian posse traced him north a few

155

miles, then lost him. He may have gone into the Pinoleño mountains for a quick hideout."

Barnes was silent again. Then he said, "Cap, what are you leading up to?"

"You."

"Me? Cap, I was his partner. And I owe him my life."

"And you're the one who knows him best—his habits, how he will act in most circumstances."

"How do they know it was Kenton?"

"Bank manager recognized him. Had met him once in the past."

"No face covering?"

"Neckerchief, but it slipped during the melee."

"Cap, get somebody else. I refuse the assignment."

There was a pause, then Ryerson said, "Think about this: Kenton's needless killing of wanted men was bad enough, but now he's killing law-abiding citizens. He's an outlaw now, a dangerous one, and there will be future killings unless you stop him."

"Me?"

"Arrest him. Bring him in to stand trial. That's what I'm asking."

"You know better, Cap. You think he's the kind to submit to arrest?"

"To you he might."

"Slim chance."

"Take it. You may save the lives of a lot of innocent victims." Ryerson paused. "You may be saving his life, too."

At Willcox Barnes debarked and saw to the unloading of his horse and pack mule.

He went at once to the site of the bank robbery, and was greeted somewhat suspiciously by the manager, who happened to be near his entrance as he entered.

The man kept peering over Barnes's shoulder at the animals he had tied up outside.

Barnes produced his identification and badge for him to examine.

After a study of these credentials, the banker's manner eased. He said, "You'll have to make some allowances for my leeriness of strangers. I witnessed most of the slaughter from my rear office, a few days back. The robber—killer—rode off with his take on a horse he'd hitched exactly where your own is now standing."

"It must have been a shocking experience."

"Four of my employees shot to death—because one produced a pistol as the robber was making his exit. The bastard halted in his tracks, right there in the doorway, and coolly killed the one with the gun, then the other three for no reason at all. A terrible thing—terrible!"

"I understand," Barnes said. "I have witnessed such during my career as a ranger." He was thinking back to Jake's massacre of the four rustlers in the saloon down in Cocóspera.

"I hope I never see such a thing again," the banker said.

"I've been told he was last seen heading north toward the Pinoleños."

"We thought so. But there's an update on that. He was reported seen near Steele's Station. Must have veered westward a little. The guess now is that he had in mind the Galiuros."

"Wild and rugged country," Barnes said. "A high range of mountains."

"So I've heard," the banker said. "Must be game to hunt up there. Could be a place a man would pick, was he wanting to lay low for a spell."

"I'll look into it," Barnes said.

Steele's Station was a now-deserted swing station for a forgotten stage line once used by early prospectors feeling their way into the southern end of the Galiuros.

It was sometimes inhabited by a hermit wanderer, as a refuge from the weather for himself and his burro.

It was luck that Barnes caught him there. Like a lot of old prospectors, he was a willing talker.

"Yep, I seen him," the old man said.

"How do you know it was him?" Barnes said.

"I didn't until I went into Willcox for supplies, a day after. Town was in a uproar, all about the bank robbing and the killing by the son of a bitch. Somebody give me the description of a bank feller who survived had told. Fit this bastard to a tee."

"Describe him to me."

"Hard-enough-looking hombre about your age. Riding a blue roan horse and leading a pack mule. You a lawman?"

"Ranger."

"One of them, huh? Well, what I hear about your kind, you're hell on outlaws. But let me tell you, this one looked like one bad hombre to tangle with." The old man gestured toward the mountain rising nearby. "You ever been in them Galureeze?"

"Galureeze?" Barnes said. "You mean Galiuros?"

"Around here we call them the Galureeze."

"Who does?" Barnes said.

"Nowadays," the old man said, "only me, I reckon." He paused. "So you figure to go into them after that killing bastard?"

"Is that where he went?"

"Where else? A killer wanting to hide out, he couldn't find rougher country to do it."

Barnes was thoughtful, then said, "You've been in there?"

"Why you asking?"

"I could use a guide."

"I been there, but not lately. My age, it's too damn rough for me. And especial I wouldn't go after a bastard, bloody

as this one is. I leave such jobs for you rangers. I'm aiming
to live to be a old man."

"Where's the place to start?"

"Go west a bit. There's a canyon splits the toe of the
range. There's an old Apache trail runs north over and
through some of the most chopped-up, hard-going climbing country in the world. Was a time the Aravaipa Apaches
took it when on the run from army units." He paused.
"Stopped the army every time, I reckon."

Barnes got in his saddle, and picked up the pack animal's line, ready to leave.

"He's got several days' lead on you," the old man said.
"But he may be holing up, waiting for the hell he stirred
up to die down."

"I hope so," Barnes said.

"You do? By God, was me, I'd be hoping otherwise," the
old man said. "He ain't the kind I'd want to tangle with."

There was a stream flowing out of a canyon bottom, with
cottonwoods along the banks. He found a trail here and
some faint hoofprints that indicated the passage of a rider.
A little farther on were dried droppings, probably several
days old.

Within a few miles there were sycamores and alders, and
above him on one side was visible a rimrock several hundred feet high.

An indication of rugged country ahead, he thought.

Dusk was falling in the canyon and he made camp for
the night.

In the morning he found the trace climbing and two
hours of riding brought him to a deserted cabin located
above yet another canyon. A few chunks of ore were scattered about, evidence that this might have once been the
base for an early prospector.

Beyond here he lost the trail, and spent considerable
time relocating it.

He was close now to what could be the toughest peak of the Galiuros. He could see stands of juniper and ponderosa pine on its slopes.

Skirting over an escarpment, he lost the trail again and again as it threaded its way through dense stands of manzanita and piñon.

It came to him then that Kenton might have no intention of stopping, that he might be using the old Aravaipa trail as a means to disappear from the earth as far as Willcox area searchers were concerned. If it hadn't been for the chance reporting of the old wanderer at Steele's Station, the ruse could have worked.

Certainly there was plenty of game in here to exist on. He had seen antelope sign several times and a bighorn sheep grazing on a rimrock edge. Twice he had seen black bears and glimpsed from a distance what he made out to be a mountain lion; he heard wolves. All of which indicated an adequate food source for predators.

Including Kenton, he thought wryly. A predator was what Jake had become.

He came upon a campsite he judged had been Kenton's several nights past. By this he guessed that if Kenton had not lingered in the range he would be long out of it by now.

He felt an urgency to hurry, but the roughness of the twisting faint trail prevented it.

Eventually he reached a cross-canyon divide, climbed a steep side just east of another towering peak, and descended into a stretch of pine where the ground was less rocky and the way was plainer.

And here, lulled by the brief respite, he was surprised to come face to face with a man armed with a rifle, standing in his way.

"You hold it, hear me!" the man said. Barnes heard the trace of an accent, possibly Scandinavian.

He halted.

"What you been doing here?"

"Passing through," Barnes said.

"Nobody pass through here. What for?"

Barnes chose not to answer.

"You been second man come through. I think you spy on me."

"Why would I?" Barnes said.

"You like everybody, after gold maybe."

"You a prospector?"

"I don't tell you."

Barnes decided he probably was, from his accusatory tone.

Barnes said, "You say another man came through. How long ago?"

"I think maybe a week."

"You stop him too?"

"I only see him too far to shoot. He don't see me."

"You're lucky," Barnes said.

"Lucky?"

"He's a killer," Barnes said. "Robbed the bank in Willcox. Shot four men dead."

The man lost his truculence. "Oh, my!"

"Oh, my! is right."

"You try to catch killer?"

Barnes produced his silver star and showed it. "Arizona Ranger," he said.

The man lowered his rifle. "I hear good thing, your kind."

"I'm glad of that," Barnes said.

"How much that bad man he get?"

"The bank isn't saying. Why do you ask?"

"I just been think how much I get if shoot that bad feller."

"Too late now," Barnes said.

"Yah, for me," the Scandinavian said. "But you, ranger, you go, maybe shoot him dead."

The words somehow bothered Barnes, and he did not

answer. He gave a short nod and passed on as the man moved aside.

He went for several miles, but never saw any sign of the prospector's living quarters. Nor did he see horse or pack animal. Yet he had the feeling his questioner was a permanent resident of an otherwise uninhabited terrain.

But he knew from experience that these solitary searchers for riches might be found anywhere. To Barnes, who had encountered many of them over the years, they always seemed a race apart.

So thinking, he made a final camp as evening fell, but built no fire. There was always a chance that Kenton had chosen this northern end of the range for a layover before venturing out.

This kept him on edge, so that he awoke often, alert for sight or sound of danger.

Eventually first light came, and he broke camp, did without coffee, and munched some jerky as he continued on. The terrain was as gnarly as ever until he reached an easterly creek bottom that eventually skirted a steep, rocky hill and left the last wild end of the range. Ahead lay what he guessed to be the upper Avaraipa Valley.

A damn hard ride for nothing, he thought, and rode out on the valley floor.

There was graze land here, and the trail ended as he reached it. Grama grass had obliterated any trace that might have existed earlier, and it grew heavy enough to cover any recent passage of a single rider and pack animal.

Off to the north a few miles, according to his map, curved Aravaipa Creek. Would Kenton head that way? The creek went northwesterly, then veered west to eventually reach the San Pedro River.

A short distance east rose the Pinaleños; Kenton had turned away from them earlier, and it wasn't likely he'd go toward them now. To the southeast forty or fifty miles was

Willcox, and Barnes was damned sure Jake wouldn't be heading back there.

He made his decision then, to follow the Aravaipa to the San Pedro.

There was a town or two along the river. There might even be a telephone from which he could call headquarters to make a report. Not that it was something he relished doing, considering it appeared Kenton had got away clean so far.

But there was always the chance he might encounter Kenton over there someplace.

It was dusk when he reached the river. There was a cluster of shacks here at the confluence with the creek. Lamplight showed in one structure, and as he neared he saw it was a store of sorts.

He tied up the tired animals and moved to enter.

On impulse he pinned his star on his coat.

As he stepped in, a man seated in a chair behind a counter looked up from a newspaper he'd been reading.

His eyes took in Barnes's badge at once. He nodded a greeting.

"Looking for someone, ranger?"

"What gives you that idea?" Barnes said.

"Mostly this newspaper I'm reading. About a week or so old, but I just got it. Dropped off by a feller coming this way from Dudleyville. All about the bank robbery and killing over in Willcox."

"It was a pretty scary crime," Barnes said.

"Would've been a hell of a lot scarier for me had I knowed I was maybe talking to the bastard that done it, a few days back."

"He came through here then?"

"Jasper that fits the newspaper description did. So did the hoss he rode. A blue roan."

"That's him," Barnes said.

"A man in the outlaw business, wanting to make a getaway, I don't understand his choices of hosses," the store-keeper said.

"How's that?"

"I mean a blue roan is some scarcer than a lot of other colors, ain't it? Why pick one if you don't want to be easy identified?"

"It can work both ways," Barnes said. "Believe me, this Kenton isn't a fool. Now he's got folks looking for a standout-color horse, he'll be switching mounts soon as he gets the chance."

"I never thought of it that way," the storekeeper said. "You reckon he does that, you won't know him if you catch him?"

"I'll know him," Barnes said. "No matter what color the horse."

"He left here going south. Next town is Redington, got a fair sized livery stable there. Likely place to trade horses, has he so got the mind."

"I'll camp here tonight," Barnes said, "and light out that way in the morning."

"Don't see how you figure to catch up with him."

"I will," Barnes said. "Sooner or later."

Barnes rode up to the Redington livery, and the ostler came out.

He'd decided to wear his star in plain sight, figuring it easier to elicit information, assuming the people he inter-rogated were honest and law abiding.

"You happen to have bought or traded for a blue roan horse lately?" was his first question.

"You wanting to buy one?"

Barnes shrugged.

"Yeah," the ostler said. "I got a good one recent."

"What reason did the owner give for trading?"

"Said his mount was tired, wanted a fresh one."

"You know who he was?"

"Hell, no. Just another range hand, as far as I was concerned. Was he somebody?"

"He robbed the bank at Willcox. Maybe you read about it."

"Ain't read none about it," the livery man said. "Heard mention some by word of mouth." He paused, then said, "Jeez! I didn't know! That was *him*?"

"What kind of horse he trade for?"

"Went out of here riding a plain bay gelding. Picked one looked like a million others."

"Thanks," Barnes said.

"Hell," the ostler said, "you wasn't interested in buying at all."

"That I wasn't," Barnes said.

"Well, good luck. You ain't but a day or so behind him."

He took to the trail again, figuring to reach Benson next day.

The last thing the ostler had said was bothering him. How could Jake be only a day or so ahead of him?

What had delayed him?

Whatever it was, he determined to take advantage of it. He'd ride until dark, start again at first light, and hope to cut Kenton's lead even more.

CHAPTER 18

NOW SOUTH OF Benson, Kenton believed his best hope was to run for the border again.

After leaving the Galiuros and following Aravaipa Creek to the river where he had spoken with the storekeeper, he had pretended to ride south. But once out of sight, he'd turned north, bound for Dudleyville and parts beyond.

But what he'd encountered in Dudleyville had made him change his mind about fleeing in that direction.

The first thing he saw there was a wanted poster with his name on it. It described him as the man who had robbed and killed at Willcox. It was the first he was sure that he'd been identified.

The poster had been displayed inside a general store on the outskirts of town, which he had entered to replenish his provisions.

It startled him, but was not enough in itself to change his destination.

Then, as he glanced over the dodger, the proprietor struck up a conversation. "Five hundred dollars reward there."

"So I see," Kenton said. The man's manner was similar to what he had often noticed during his career as a lawman. There were people who would astound you by their lack of suspicion of strangers who presented a casual demeanor.

He crossed over to the counter and said, "I need provisions."

"What I'm here for," the storekeeper said.

One of those chubby and cheerful ones, Kenton thought, lucky for me.

"Traveling," the storekeeper said. "Since I'm located here at the south end of town, and you're making your first stop here. I'd say you're on you're way northward."

Kenton was silent.

"How's that for detective work, friend?"

"Great," Kenton said.

"Kind of a hobby of mine."

"Nice hobby," Kenton said, then rattled off a short list of supplies he wanted.

The merchant busied himself getting them, but continued to talk. "Feller come in earlier today, just down from up north, Roosevelt way, and said them dodgers is out in every town from there to here."

"Outlaws nowadays are having it tough," Kenton said. "With the rangers giving them hell everywhere."

He paid for the provisions and gathered them up.

"Nice talking to you," the storekeeper said.

"Yeah," Kenton said, "same here."

Once mounted he had ridden north again, but only for a short distance. He then reversed his direction. Thirty miles south to Redington. Then thirty more. Here he was, south of Benson, and thinking he'd have less risk in Mexico if he went deep enough into it. Get far south of Sonora someplace. Durango, maybe. With the five thousand dollars American he could live high for a long time down there.

He was still following the course of the river as he approached the Fairbank area. Here he realized that keeping on would bring him eventually to the border above Morelos again where a short time past he had escaped Soto's Rurales.

To veer eastward would bring him closer to Naco, where a ranger was usually posted.

He decided to work his way southwest toward the trail that led down to Lochiel, where he had crossed with

Barnes so many weeks ago. Far enough to be away from both Naco to the east and Nogales to the west.

It was a crossing not too closely watched by law enforcers.

Barnes rode into Benson and inquired around just long enough to find a couple of men who'd seen a rider go through, two or three days back, who fit the description he gave them.

"Rode out of town, going south," one of them said.

Barnes pushed on.

Luck was with him again at Fairbank. Here he had been not only seen, but recognized.

"Sure," a native said. "I saw him and remembered seeing him as a ranger, with you, in Douglas. Hell, I didn't know he was now a wanted man."

"Damn!" Barnes said to himself. "Don't anybody ever look at the dodgers posted around here?"

"He went out of here west along the tracks," the native said. "And him being on the run, he might have had it in mind to take the trail down to Lochiel. You ride west like he went, you'll come to it south of the railroad. There's some cattle-loading chutes there, used sometimes by ranchers from the Elgin area want to ship beef."

Barnes gave his thanks and started off. He was almost out of earshot when the informant hollered, "What made a ranger turn bad?"

Barnes didn't answer. Hell, he didn't know.

He turned into the train station and called Ryerson to report where he was and where he was going.

"Kenton's on his way toward Santa Cruz County," he told the captain. Might be going for the crossing down at Lochiel.

"I'll alert the sheriff to get over there to cover it," Ryerson said.

*   *   *

Sergeant Soto, in Mexican Nogales, had waited with fuming impatience while Sheriff Castillo in American Nogales tried to obtain a clearance for him and his Rurales to enter gringo territory.

But when Castillo's efforts failed, he hid his anger.

He had intentions of his own, but said, "For now, I have just received orders from Colonel Kosterlitzky to return to Magdalena."

Then Castillo had said, "Too bad. I've just had a call from the ranger captain, telling me he believes Kenton is in my county and heading for the border because he is now badly wanted in Arizona for a crime committed there."

"I will tell the colonel," Soto said.

"Tell him it would be best if you and your men took a position in the area south of Lochiel."

"I will tell him that also," Soto said.

One of Soto's men overheard his end of the phone conversation within the cramped quarters where the three wounded men had been convalescing, while the other two had gone to Magdalena. Everyone's injuries had healed pretty well now.

"*Que pasa, jefe?*" he asked Soto, eyeing him curiously as he hung up the phone.

"That Castillo," he said. "He tells me that the *cabrón* Kenton is on the way to the border and that it would be good for us to wait in the area of Lochiel in case he slips across."

"And what will Castillo do?"

"I do not think that gringo-ized sheriff has tried as much as he could to get us a permit to enter Arizona. What he really wants is to capture Kenton himself and make a trial, to gather glory for his next election campaign. He will wait at Lochiel."

"I would like to get my hands on that *cabrón* Kenton," the Rurale said.

"And I," the other said.

"It makes us three," Soto said. "And if Castillo is the one to succeed, it would cheat us of our rightful revenge."

"What can we do, *jefe*?"

"We are going to go up north of the line," Soto said.

"Ilegally, *jefe*?"

"We are going to cross and go up the trail a ways to wait. North of where Castillo waits. So he cannot cheat us. And we will give that *cabrón* a trial of our own. Rurale style."

Instead of going west along the tracks to reach the railhead junction with the Lochiel trail, Kenton had ridden southwest along a minor trace he thought would be a shortcut. Deep into a confusing maze of hills and canyons, it soon petered out and left him fighting the twisting terrain to maintain his direction.

It was slow going and he made a cold camp at dark, cursing the choice he had made. He lost a full day's time before he eventually broke out into country that looked familiar somewhere below Elgin.

The trail here was easy, and his mount was tired from nearly two days of hard going, so he let it have its head.

He dozed in the saddle.

They caught him thus. Asleep and awakened by the sound of Spanish-accented words of threat.

"Wake up, you *hijo de puta*!"

Soto and two of his Rurales were spaced out around him at a few yards distance, mounted and with pistols pointed.

The sergeant, directly in front, was the one who spoke. He was staring at him with hatred on his face.

"So! Gringo *bastardo*."

Kenton's mind raced. In their hands he was dead, and he knew it.

"Draw your *pistola*," Soto said. "Slow and easy, and drop it."

That wasn't Kenton's way. He drew, but not slow. His

gun was up and cocked and ready to fire at Soto when a shot by a Rurale on his right side drove it from his hand.

The shot left him disarmed and with numbed fingers, but his adrenaline was pumping, and he drove spurs into his mount and charged directly at Soto.

Soto, his gun at the ready, dropped his aim slightly and shot the horse point blank into its heart. The horse went down to its knees, then toppled sideways as Kenton struggled loose from the stirrups and saddle to avoid being crushed.

He now stood defenseless beside his dying mount and looked up at Soto.

"You dumb Mexican son of a bitch," he said. "You could have as easy shot me as the horse."

"I still can," Soto said, "but I have another plan instead." He turned to one of his men who had a folding, army-type trench shovel tied to his saddle.

"Jesús," he said to the man. "Unfold the shovel and place it in his hands."

Jesús dismounted to do so and held the shovel out toward Kenton. Kenton was massaging his stinging hand. He made no move to take it.

"Take it," Soto said. "It is for to dig a grave."

Kenton understood, but something made him say, "A small shovel to bury a dead horse."

"But big enough for a dead gringo, no?" Soto paused. "It is often a way we have for criminals in Mexico. You get to dig your own."

"I'm damned if I will!"

"Take the shovel from Jesús, gringo," Soto said. "Feel lucky. You know what the name Jesús means in English? It means Jesus. Not many times does Jesus attend a burial in person."

"Some joke," Kenton said. "But I'm not digging any grave."

*   *   *

Sheriff Castillo had ridden fast to reach Lochiel. He wanted to make certain he was there if Kenton came that way. It would be a big coup for his reputation if he could personally take him.

He arrived, somewhat tired from his ride. Too much desk work, he was thinking. He had been an active deputy around Santa Cruz County in earlier years and really preferred that life to what he did now. But it was matter of pride to his Hispanic blood that he had reached the position he now had. And he hoped here to add to it.

It was a blow to his plan when he was acosted by a resident who knew him, and informed that an outlying rancher had been in with a wild story of seeing Mexicans in Rurale garb moving north of the Washington Camp road above the border.

He started up the Lochiel trace at once.

Barnes knew he was following a rider by only a short distance, indicated by the recent horse droppings he was coming upon.

He had first encountered them several miles back, as he passed the last of a range of hills bordering the trail on the east. He had no way of knowing who the rider might be, but he paced his mount a little faster and believed he was drawing closer.

And then, abruptly, as he rode out of a bend in the trail, he came upon a scene that shocked him.

Sergeant Soto and two of his Rurales stood in firing-squad-formation facing Jake Kenton, who stood twenty yards away on the edge of a narrow coulee. Two of the Rurales held carbines; Soto, his pistol.

Barnes could see they had tethered their horses to some bushes, out of the way of their target.

Soto, his voice carrying, was now venting his last-minute feelings on Jake.

"So you refuse the ritual of digging your own grave.

Well, that ditch will do as well. But do not believe we will cover your body. Perhaps the coyotes that eat your flesh will cover your bones with their excrement."

"Go to hell!" Kenton shouted back.

"*Listo!*" Soto yelled.

He and his men cocked their weapons.

"*Apunten!*"

They aimed at Kenton.

Barnes was the one to fire. His shot kicked up dirt at their feet and made them swerve their guns toward him.

They fired in panic and missed, as he yelled, "I am the American law!"

At that moment Soto remembered their intended victim, and threw a panicked glance at where Kenton had been standing.

When he saw nothing, his eyes went to the horses tied to the bushes farther down the ditch.

He was in time to glimpse Kenton reach for and jerk a horse's reins loose from its tie, and disappear down into the coulee, only to show head and shoulders again as he mounted.

Soto fired a revolver shot that missed, but it halted Kenton, who turned in the saddle, drew a sheathed carbine, and shot Soto through the chest.

Soto went down, blood spurting from his wound.

His men, now ignoring Barnes, rushed to his side.

Barnes came up then, as Kenton disappeared.

On Soto's horse, and with Soto's carbine.

CHAPTER 19

DESPITE THE PAIN and shock of a critical wound, Soto was filled with anger. He looked up at Barnes, who was bent over him, and met his eyes.

"It was because of you he got away," he said.

"You can't execute a man that way," Barnes said. "Not in my country."

Soto looked at the ranger star he was wearing. "I remember you from that time near Cocóspera. And you are the partner of that son of a whore."

"Was," Barnes said. "You must have heard his star was taken from him."

"Then why did you save his life just now?"

It was a logical question to ask, Barnes thought.

Why, indeed?

It was the same old feeling of a debt owed. A feeling he thought he'd shaken.

He couldn't explain that to the Rurale sergeant. He couldn't explain it to himself.

Soto said one more thing before he passed out. "Why you don't go after him?"

"I will," Barnes said.

Then seeing Soto was unconscious he said to the Rurales, "Without a doctor, I think he will die."

The one called Jesús nodded. *"Un médico, sí."*

"It is best that you take him to Lochiel, then send to Nogales for one," Barnes said.

"We will try," Jesús said. "You, *rangero,* you will pursue that *bastardo* as you told the *jefe*? For what he done?"

174

"For what he did here and elsewhere," Barnes said. He went to his horse and swung up.

The two Rurales looked up at him with skepticism. Neither spoke.

Barnes could understand their mistrust. It was because of him that Kenton had got away, and that their sergeant lay bleeding and could very likely die.

He turned his horse and rode southward in the direction he judged Kenton had gone, half-expecting—until he was out of their sight—a bullet in his back.

Sheriff Castillo was hurrying up the trace, trying to overtake the Rurales. Two thoughts were in his mind: He had to prevent them from taking any action on Santa Cruz soil, lest he come under censure for allowing such to occur in his jurisdiction. And akin to that, he had to prevent them from taking Kenton, because he wanted that action, for political reasons, to be his own.

The tracks of Soto and two riders were easy enough to follow once they cut in above the Washington Camp trail. It appeared there had been little recent traffic on the trace, but Castillo kept his eyes busy reading sign to see if Soto had turned off anywhere.

And thus he came upon the prints of a rider coming south that suddenly vanished. A brief scrutiny quickly picked out where they had turned off toward the west.

He sat there a short while contemplating this.

He was about to move on when he saw Barnes coming toward him.

The ranger stopped short at the sight of him, then approached slowly as he waited.

Reaching him, Barnes said, "Sheriff."

"Barnes, isn't it?"

Barnes nodded.

"You on Kenton's trail?"

"Yeah."

Castillo was silent a moment before he said, "So am I."

Barnes gestured at the southbound hoofprints. "Those are his."

"You sure?"

"I'm sure. Been following them a spell."

"From where?"

Barnes quickly sketched in what had happened with the Rurales.

Castillo sat transfixed as he began, and only when Barnes ended with the words, "So Soto is down and out of it," did the sheriff relax. Then he said, "Kenton's heading into the Patagonia range now, I'd say." He pointed to where the tracks had turned west.

"Why?"

"Hell, man, it's good hideout in those mountains from somebody like Soto who don't know them."

"I told you Soto's badly wounded."

"But Kenton couldn't know that if he left as fast as you say. He'd expect the Rurales to be hounding him still, and for him to keep trying for Mexico would be foolish now."

"Yeah, I guess."

"And with mining spots, places like Harshaw in the Patagonias, he can buy grub if he needs it."

Barnes was silent, weighing the sheriff's words, hesitating because he did not know Castillo well.

Castillo waited for a long moment, then impatiently heeled his horse and moved onto the new tracks. He paused there, looked back, and said, "You coming?"

"Yeah," Barnes said, and fell in behind him.

They rode the miles in silence and entered the scrub oak country of the low reaches of the Patagonias.

They came upon a well-used trail, and Castillo said, "Bound for Harshaw."

"Looks so," Barnes said.

They came to the settlement: a sprawl of wooden shacks,

a few brick buildings, and a cemetery on an adjoining slope.

Castillo appeared familiar with it and made his way to a small office bearing the sign CONSTABLE on it. Beneath it in small letters was a name, Joe Eakus.

He and Barnes dismounted and went in.

Eakus was a stockily built man of forty, pale skinned as a miner.

He looked up from a battered desk and showed recognition as his eyes met Castillo's. He stood, and extended his hand.

"Glad to see you, Sheriff."

"Likewise, Eakus. This is Ranger Barnes."

"Damned glad to see you both," Eakus said. Then, before Castillo could speak again, he said, "I'd have been even more glad had you got here a hour or so ago."

"Trouble, Eakus?" Castillo said.

"No," Eakus said. "But only because I made a point to avoid it."

Barnes was watching his face and could see a mixture of regret and shame touch it as he said, "Jake Kenton came through."

"You recognized him?" Castillo said.

"Well, I got a dodger description here, and it sure as hell fit." He paused. "Anyhow, I got it in my head it was him. Enough to make me lose my sand." His pale face flushed. "I admit it. Hell, they made me constable here because nobody else would take the job. More money in mine work, but my health was getting bad." He paused. "I ain't got what it takes to be a lawman, and I realize it now."

"You talk to him?" Barnes said.

"No. But I was in the hardware when he come in and bought a handgun to fill an empty holster. Reason I took notice of him at first was the way he kept looking at this here constable badge I'm wearing. Made me nervous. Then he left, got on his horse, and rode up toward the high ground. It was then I come back to the office and refreshed my memory on the wanted sheet."

Barnes and Castillo were both silent.

Their silence seemed to agitate Eakus. His features reddened again, and he said, "I been sitting here calling myself names ever since."

"It's just as well you did it the way you did," Barnes said. "He's quick to kill when he's crossed."

"So I read," Constable Eakus said.

They left the settlement on a westward trace that Eakus had said he thought Kenton might have taken.

"An old prospecting trail," he said. "It'll peter out after a bit. But it'll start him out toward the peaks if he has the idea of shaking you off."

They found Kenton's fresh tracks, which continued on as the constable had suggested.

The trail twisted and climbed, heading toward the distant summit of the range.

Barnes said, "You know something of these mountains. You think he's figuring on crossing them?"

"Could be. There's a place called Ambush Pass up there someplace."

After a while Castillo said, "Judging by the freshess of those hoofprints, he don't seem to be in no hurry."

Barnes was bothered by that, but he said nothing.

They pushed on. Later they stopped to rest the horses. There was manzanita here, scrub oak, and some piñon, but no tall growth, and they could look up and study the heights.

Barnes said, "If he's looking down he can see us."

"He could be over the summits by now."

"Unless he stopped to wait," Barnes said.

"Why would he do that?"

"He's not of a nature to run. If he sees pursuit, he's likely to stop and confront it."

Castillo was silent a moment before he spoke. Then he said, "Listen, ranger, we got to work together to get him."

Barnes said nothing.

"You understand, *amigo*? Like you and me been long-time partners."

When Barnes made no comment, Castillo gave him a searching look and said, "You got to forget that you and him used to work together."

Barnes knew that fact was bothering the sheriff. Castillo was scared.

Barnes was still silent.

Castillo took on a hard scowl. He said, "You been listening to what I say?"

"I heard."

"Then you better not forget," the sheriff said. "You give him a chance, we'll both be dead."

When the shot came, they were exiting a narrow canyon, and it was by chance that Barnes was ahead by several yards.

Or was it? Castillo had seemed to drop behind slightly as they approached the entrance, making it natural enough for Barnes to lead.

It was a warning shot, Barnes thought. A miss that struck to one side of his mount, kicking up dirt and gravel.

It came from the heights. Jake could shoot better than that with a rifle.

By reflex though, Barnes whirled his horse around and retreated into the canyon on the heels of Castillo.

They halted behind a rock-strewn turn in the cut, and Castillo said, "That was a near miss!"

"Maybe," Barnes said. "He always was best with a revolver."

"You think he meant to miss?"

Barnes shrugged. "Who knows?"

"Listen," Castillo said, "we can't go forward here." He

was appraising the slope contours on either side of the canyon. "We got to go back to where we can climb out, one on each of those escarpments."

"And then?" Barnes said.

"There's some timber growth there for cover. We make our way up and try to flank him."

"All right," Barnes said.

Castillo was already headed for the right side of the canyon, which was here comparatively shallow.

Barnes took the left side, and started the climb, leading his horse.

The sheriff reached the rounded rim first, and when Barnes reached the top and looked across he saw him waiting. For a moment they stared at each other, then each turned, mounted his horse, and began to make his way upward again.

From a ledge above, Kenton had seen them disappear back into the canyon after his warning shot.

Briefly he castigated himself for his deliberate miss. He must be getting soft.

Why did he spare Wes, when it was to his advantage to kill him?

He did not have a ready answer.

And now, with his targets gone from sight, he allowed himself to ponder this.

It was unlike him, and it bothered him.

But he'd felt he had to do it.

But abruptly, as he glimpsed his pursuers climb out of the canyon bottom, far below and out of weapon range, he again understood one thing: He had to kill them before they killed him.

He was bothered again by a thought. For the first time in years, he was going to find that hard to do.

For the first time since before he'd killed at Las Guásimas.

*   *   *

The growth on the side Castillo was ascending was heavier than that on Barnes's. Barnes, glancing across the canyon to mark his progress, had only occasional glimpses of him, but saw he had drawn ahead.

Upward, through the thinner screening on his own side, Barnes could now see Kenton waiting on a ledge above the head of the canyon, staring down at him.

They were in plain sight of each other. But not within effective rifle range.

The way Jake was watching him, he seemed unaware that Castillo was climbing the other shoulder.

Was there a chance he would submit to arrest? Barnes wondered. Even an outside chance? He had the urge to find out. Anything was possible.

He halted, tied his neckerchief to his rifle barrel and waved it in a sign to ask for a parley.

Kenton did not move for a long moment; then, to Barnes's hopeful surprise, he held up his own weapon in the same way and signaled acceptance.

Barnes hesitated, then moved upward, hoping for the best. He still had that much trust in Kenton. He looked once, but could no longer see Castillo. Then he kept his eyes on the ledge where Kenton was.

There were times when he lost sight of it from where the timber grew thicker, but periodically he could see Jake still waiting for him. He's trusting me, too, Barnes thought. Comes from our long association.

Then he thought again of Castillo and searched the opposite slope. There he was now, within good range of the ledge, rifle aimed upward; Barnes knew he was targeting an unsuspecting Jake.

He reacted without thought, driven by feeling, to stop Castillo from firing, and jerked his own rifle around for a snap shot in Castillo's direction.

The shot, deliberately low, struck rock and ricocheted up to strike Castillo's forearm.

Castillo's weapon went tumbling toward the canyon rim and over the precipice. It left Castillo armed with only a revolver, at rifle range of either man.

He started to flee for thicker cover, and as he ran, Kenton shot from above and dropped him.

Barnes saw it happen, heard Jake continue to fire, saw his shots kick up dirt around the fallen sheriff as Castillo tried to crawl toward hiding.

A second passed as Barnes hesitated, his rifle now swinging to point at Jake. A second to make a decision that was almost too late.

He squeezed the trigger and thought he'd missed. Jake's rifle slid from his hands but he still stood erect, staring down at Wes, and even at that range Barnes imagined he saw reproach in Jake's eyes.

Then Jake toppled forward over the ledge, shattering his skull on a bed of rocks below.

They left his body there. It was impossible for Barnes to retrieve it without help. Castillo was badly wounded in the leg by Kenton's shot, with a lesser one in his arm from Barnes's ricochet. He urgently needed medical attention.

Castillo managed, with Barnes's help, to mount his horse, and they rode down the mountain, heading back toward Harshaw.

At first Castillo griped about the ricochet.

"It was your bullet that kept me from getting that bastard."

"That I intended," Barnes said. "We had a truce to parley."

"Even so. You know damn well he wouldn't have given up."

"I had to give him the chance."

Castillo rode in silence for a while, thinking about this.

Then he said, "I guess maybe I understand how that could be, after how it once was between you."

Barnes did not answer, and they rode again without speaking.

When Castillo spoke again, he said, "I got to thank you for stopping him from killing me while I was crawling."

"I had to do that too," Barnes said.

Castillo was a thoughtful man. "Still, it must've been hard," he said after a while.

He'd never know how hard, Barnes thought.

If you have enjoyed this book and would like to receive details on other Walker Western titles, please write to:

Western Editor
Walker and Company
435 Hudson Street
New York, NY 10014

Last one 2/00